The
Little Ballerina and
Her Dancing
Horse

Also by Gelsey Kirkland
and Greg Lawrence:

DANCING ON MY GRAVE
THE SHAPE OF LOVE

The Little Ballerina and Her Dancing Horse

Gelsey Kirkland and Greg Lawrence

DOUBLEDAY

NEW YORK   LONDON   TORONTO   SYDNEY   AUCKLAND

PUBLISHED BY DOUBLEDAY
a division of
Bantam Doubleday Dell Publishing Group, Inc.
1540 Broadway, New York, New York 10036

DOUBLEDAY and the portrayal of an anchor with a dolphin are
trademarks of Doubleday, a division of Bantam Doubleday Dell
Publishing Group, Inc.

Library of Congress Cataloging-in-Publication Data

Kirkland, Gelsey.
The little ballerina and her dancing horse / Gelsey Kirkland and
Greg Lawrence ; [illustrated by Jacqueline Rogers]. — 1st ed.
    p.   cm.
  Summary: Eleven-year-old Rosie must choose between the two
things she loves most—ballet and horseback riding.
  [1. Ballet dancing—Fiction. 2. Horsemanship—Fiction.
3. Horses—Fiction.] I. Lawrence, Greg. II. Rogers, Jacqueline,
ill. III. Title.
PZ7.K63465Si   1993
[Fic]—dc20   93-20355
                                                           CIP
                                                            AC

ISBN 0-385-46978-0
Text copyright © 1993 by Gelsey Kirkland and Greg Lawrence
Illustrations copyright © 1993 by Jacqueline Rogers

Book Design by Gretchen Achilles.

Acknowledgments

My husband and I wish to thank Steve Rubin and his good offices at Doubleday. We owe a longstanding debt of gratitude to our editors, Jacqueline Onassis and Bruce Tracy, and to Shaye Areheart for her help at the start.

We are grateful to the following for all of their support, advice, and encouragement: my mother, Nancy Salisbury; my sister, Johana McHugh; my brothers, Marshall and Christopher Kirkland; my sister-in-law, Paula Stricklin; Peter Stelzer; Allison Stelzer; Peter and Judith Wyer; Bonnie Egan; David Howard; Barna Ostertag; Pilar Garcia Sussman; Deane Rink; Tamie Lynn; Zesna Bozick; Marysarah Quinn; and Scott Moyers. Special inspiration was also provided by my nieces: Chloe, Delta, and Olivia.

The
Little Ballerina and
Her Dancing
Horse

Chapter 1

My friend, Emily, says I'm ballet crazy and horse crazy too. She says that because I'm crazy about dancing and riding. But I found out if you love to dance and ride as much as I do, it can make you really crazy. Like if you have to decide which one you love more, or which one you'd rather do after school. I mean sometimes when I'm in my ballet class, I think I might rather be riding. But then other times when I go riding, I think I might rather be dancing. Emily says I think too much, but lots of times I don't know what I think and can't decide.

My name is Rosalie, but everybody calls me Rosie for short. I don't know why my parents didn't just name me Rosie, since that's what they call me most of the time anyway. I can always tell whenever they get mad or they have something really serious to talk about, because that's the only time they slip up and say Rosalie. I've already told my mom I want to change my name, but she says I'm going to have to wait until I grow up. She thinks I might change my mind someday, but I know I won't.

It's not that it's such a dumb name, but I want to be a ballerina someday—I'm sure of that—and so I have to have a name that sounds really, really good. I mean, whoever heard of a ballerina named Rosalie Daniels? I told my mom that lots of ballerinas make up names for themselves so people will remember them. Like Margot Fonteyn—she was a really famous ballerina and she made up her name. Anyway, I'm making up a list of names and writing them in my diary so I can choose my favorite one when the time comes.

I'd better tell you about my diary. My mom gave it to me for my birthday this year, when I turned eleven. It's leather with a gold clasp and key and all. I keep it in a drawer in my night table, and I never show it to anybody except for Sugar, my horse. But Sugar's my best friend in the whole world. I'd better explain about him too, because sometimes I write things for Sugar in my diary, and you might not understand. You see, we live on a farm, and my mom and dad gave me Sugar when I was about two years old. It was so long ago, I hardly remember. My dad used to take me out riding in the fields around our house before I learned how to sit up on the saddle by myself, and we used to play this game where I'd whisper into Sugar's ear and ask him which way to go. Then I'd point for my dad, and he'd tug on the reins a little, and that's the way we'd ride, with me sitting in front of him.

The thing is that I always knew what Sugar was thinking. It was just like I could read his mind, and he could read mine too, sometimes even at night when we were apart. My bedroom is on the side of our house that's right next to the barn—that's where Sugar goes to sleep at night —and from my bedroom window I can almost see the door that goes to his stall. When I'm lying in bed, I can hear him when he gets scared about something. Like if he has a bad dream, or if it thunders real loud in a lightning storm. Boy, does he go crazy when it thunders! If you live in a city, you might not know that horses scream, just like people do, when they get frightened. Sugar sounds really terrible when he screams, and he kicks his stall with his hooves. One night not long ago he had a nightmare, and the next morning my dad said, "The next time Sugar gets us up in the middle of the night, he goes to the glue factory, and that's a promise!"

The glue factory is where people send horses when nobody wants them anymore, and so I had to explain to Sugar how my dad didn't really mean what he said. Sometimes my dad gets in a bad mood, like after he wakes up in the morning, and he can be pretty touchy and say some things he doesn't mean, like that thing about the glue factory. But I knew he'd never send my horse away, not in a billion years, because my dad loves Sugar almost as much as I do. So anyhow, that afternoon I went out to the barn and climbed up the ladder to the hayloft above Sugar's stall, and I wrote him a little letter in my diary to make him feel better. It was sort of a poem with rhymes, and I read it out loud for him when I was done.

> Dear Sugar, please listen.
>> Don't believe what Dad said.
> You see, he simply woke up
>> on the wrong side of bed.
> Now you heard him promise
>> he'd turn you into glue,
> But one time he swore
>> he'd send me away too.
> We both know that Dad can get mad
>> awfully fast,
> But look at me. I'm still here!
>> His mood didn't last.
>
> The truth is that sometimes
>> when Dad comes in the house,
> I wish that he'd go far away
>> or turn into a mouse.

Of course, I don't really mean it,
　　but still it sounds bad,
And if he could hear my thoughts,
　　they might make him sad.
Oh, Sugar, I'm sure Dad loves you,
　　please have no doubt.
Mistakes are just something people
　　can't live without.

　　I could tell Sugar liked it because he put his ears back and tossed his head when I was done reading. Sometimes he does that when I dance for him. It depends, though, because sometimes horses can wake up on the wrong side of the bed too. There was a time when Sugar wasn't too crazy about my dancing, and I couldn't really blame him for feeling like he did about it because I felt almost the same way for a while. I mean I was just about ready to quit ballet forever. But that comes later. First I have to tell you about how everything started to get sort of confusing for me around here near the end of summer vacation last year, just before I went back to school.

　　It had been about the best summer I ever had. I rode Sugar almost every day, and I took ballet class three or four times a week. I also had to work for a few hours most afternoons at my father's vegetable stand down the road from our house. But I had this great deal going with my mom. She told me that if I did my chores and saved up my allowance all summer, she would help me pay for my pointe shoes. I was about to go into fifth grade, and I was supposed to start taking Miss Bradley's pointe class in the fall. I was getting pretty nervous about her class because I was old enough now that I was going to have to learn how to dance on my toes for the first time. I hadn't actually danced on pointe before, and the more I thought about it, the more I felt like I do before I take a test in school, with butterflies in my stomach and all.

Now, you might not think it, but toe shoes are awfully expensive. They cost over forty dollars a pair, and my family isn't exactly rich. When my dad heard the price, he almost had a cow. I'm not kidding. "Out of the question!" That's what he said about toe shoes. But later my mother told me she had some money put aside for a rainy day, and she promised to help me buy my toe shoes as long as I did my part. Only it had to be a big secret for a while, even from my dad. My dad's never been too keen about ballet. He wants me to be a jockey when I grow up. At least, that's what he says sometimes, because I'm short for my age and jockeys are supposed to be short.

But I don't like racing that much, and neither does Sugar, if you want to know the truth. And besides, I'm going to be taller someday. That was the whole reason I started taking ballet in the first place. When I was eight, my mother found out I was shrinking. My mom always kept track of my height. I would stand by the pantry door in the kitchen, and she'd make a mark on the edge of the door with a pencil she held across the top of my head. She did that every few months, and just before my eighth birthday those little marks started going down instead of up. I was getting shorter and shorter! My mom took me to see a doctor, and he said I had a curve in my spine.

I was either going to have to wear a crummy old brace for my back or take ballet classes. My mom took ballet when she was a girl, and she said it would improve my posture. She told my dad she would work part-time to pay for my classes, and then she got a job driving a school bus for the high school. At first my dad didn't like the idea of my mom having to work, but he finally went along with it. When he's not running the farm, he works part-time too, selling real estate. He says there's not enough money in farming anymore. My mom and dad worry a lot about money.

There was one really bad year when the harvest was so terrible we had to sell a little piece of our farm to Emily's family. I'm glad we did, though, because Emily's mom and dad built their house on the land. I don't have many friends, so it's nice to have one who lives close by. Emily takes ballet with me, but she doesn't ride because she's afraid of horses. I don't know why. Emily says she likes horses, but she's scared to go near them. I've told her how gentle Sugar is, but whenever I go riding, Emily stays home or else just watches from far away.

Anyway, at the end of the summer my mom and I had to tell my dad about the secret money that we were going to use to buy my pointe shoes. It was Labor Day weekend, and we were having dinner out on the porch because it was so hot inside the house. My dad was cooking a barbecue in the backyard, and there were these big clouds of smoke coming out of the grill. From the porch where I was, it looked for a minute like he was standing in the middle of a fire. His face was all red, and he was wearing a big floppy chef's hat and one of my mom's aprons. He had a fork in one hand and a little brush in the other, and he was putting barbecue sauce on pieces of chicken. I could tell he was in a good mood because he was whistling the whole time. My dad's a really terrific whistler. You can hear him from a mile away when he gets going.

Sherlock heard him. He's my dad's bloodhound and he's thirteen, two years older than I am, which is pretty old for a dog. He was lying in the shade under a table my mom and I were setting, and he was wagging his tail a mile a minute. We could hear that old tail of his thumping up and down on the floor. Sherlock has to be the craziest, laziest dog in the world. He didn't even bother to get up when my dad opened the screen door and walked in carrying a big plate of chicken. Sherlock just licked his chops and stretched out. He knew if he waited, my dad would feed him from the table again, even though my mom would ask my dad not to around a hundred times. The same thing happened almost every night.

All through dinner I was waiting for my mom to mention something to my dad about buying the toe shoes, but she didn't have much of a chance. My dad kept horsing around with Sherlock and telling us how he had spent the whole afternoon trying to fix the gear box of the tractor. He can usually fix anything, and he likes to brag about it. But the tractor was still sitting in the barn with parts of the motor all over the place. He said he was giving up and that he was going to have it towed to the garage in town tomorrow. My mom finally interrupted him and asked how much he thought it would cost to have fixed.

"Depends on the parts," he said. "But it shouldn't be too bad. I could do the labor myself, but I just don't have the time, not with the harvest coming in the way it is this year."

My mom looked over and gave me a little wink across the dinner table, and then she said to my dad, "I'm going to need the car tomorrow to take Rosie shopping. School starts this week, and I told her I would help pay for the toe shoes that she's been saving for."

My dad looked awfully surprised. "Toe shoes!" he said.

"I seem to remember someone telling me last year she needed a raise in her allowance so that she could save up to buy Sugar a new saddle. It's Sugar's birthday the day after tomorrow, isn't it?"

"Sugar's birthday!" I cried. "Oh, no. I can't believe it. How could I have forgotten?"

"Oh, Rosalie," said my mom, "the saddle can certainly wait until next year. You still have my old English saddle as well as your dad's Western. I'm sure you can find something nice for Sugar's birthday that won't cost too much. We can look in the tack shop tomorrow. Sugar will understand."

"But Mom," I said, "I can't keep using your saddle forever. The leather is so old that it might fall apart one day when we're riding. And I totally forgot that I promised Sugar I'd try to get a new saddle for him in time for his birthday. So I don't think he's going to understand at all."

Boy, did I feel bad all of a sudden. I couldn't even open my mouth to say anything else. My mom stood up and started clearing dishes from the table. My dad was leaning back in his chair and sort of watching her with this funny smile on his face. Then he said, "Well, I guess I don't really have anything to say about it anyway. It's Rosalie's decision, and she can spend her money on whatever she likes. But I thought she wanted her own saddle for the horse shows."

My mom said, "Rosalie, you're going to have to decide between a saddle or toe shoes. We certainly can't afford both."

After she said that, I got up fast and went straight to my room. I really wasn't too sure anymore whether I should buy a saddle or toe shoes. It was almost like I was going to have to choose between riding and dancing. I finally lay down on my bed and stared up at the ceiling, where I had this poster of Mikhail Baryshnikov jumping in the air. My life sure can get complicated sometimes. I just kept thinking to myself, how am I ever going to explain things to Sugar?

Chapter 2

The next day was Saturday, and the first thing I had to do in the morning after breakfast was clean Sugar's stall. My dad and a man from the garage were outside, hitching the tractor to a bright orange tow truck. The sun was hardly even up in the sky, and there were little wispy patches of fog over the pasture and woods behind our house. As I came down the back stairs off the porch, I saw Sherlock lying in the driveway just past where my dad was standing. That dumb old dog was chewing on one of Sugar's brushes. Boy, did I get mad. I ran right over and grabbed Sherlock by the scruff of his neck.

"You dummy," I screamed, "drop that brush!"

I tried to get Sherlock up from the ground. But he had all of this loose skin, and it just kept pulling away from his neck, like he was made of Silly Putty or something. I couldn't even budge him, and he wouldn't let go of that brush between his teeth. Sherlock nips sometimes, so I was scared to grab it away from him. He was sort of growling at me, but I couldn't tell if he really meant it or not. He kept drooling out of the side of his mouth. It was so gross. When my dad finally came to help, Sherlock looked up with those pathetic bloodshot eyes of his. Then he opened up his mouth real wide, like he was just yawning, and dropped the brush into my dad's hand.

My dad gave Sherlock a little pat on the head and said, "That's a good boy."

"Dad, how can you be nice to him?" I asked. "Look what he did to Sugar's brush!"

There were ugly teeth marks up and down the wooden handle, and some of the bristles had come off. My dad laughed and said, "Oh, simmer down, Rosalie. Somebody must have left the brush on the floor of the tack room again. Sherlock just thought it was one of his bones."

He was all wrong, of course, but I couldn't say that to my dad. Sherlock had to know Sugar's brush was no bone. He was a purebred bloodhound, so even with his eyes closed his nose could sniff out anything. But my dad let Sherlock get away with murder all the time. They were best friends, especially during hunting season. Even though Sherlock's not really a hunting dog, they went away to-gether camping and hunting every year, and the trip was a very big deal for my dad because it was the only time he didn't have to work.

So I didn't make a stink about the brush. I picked up a couple of ripe crab apples that I found in the driveway, and then I hurried inside the barn to say good morning to Sugar. I forgot to tell you how beautiful he is. He's part Arabian and has a powder-gray coat with white speckles all over his belly and back. When you rub your hand down Sugar's neck, he feels as soft as velvet. On his nose there's a streak of white that looks like a sugar cane. That's how he got his name. I gave him a big kiss on his nose and scratched behind his ears. Then I unlatched the door to his stall and went inside. I knew he'd find the apples in my pocket, and he kept nudging me until I gave them to him. Sugar loves apples, even the sour kind, but he can't eat too many because they can make him sick.

I didn't say a word to Sugar about my toe shoes or about his birthday tomorrow. What I did do was check out my mom's old English saddle. Some of the straps were frayed, and the leather looked sort of stained and splotchy. But it wasn't going to fall apart. I decided I'd clean it up and put some oil on the leather. Sooner or later I'd have to explain to Sugar that we'd have to wait a while longer for a new saddle. And I'd have to think of something really good to get him for his birthday. But at least we'd still be able to go out riding, and I could get those toe shoes that I needed for ballet class. So I could keep on riding and dancing, at least for now.

I led Sugar out to the back field to wait for me while I cleaned his stall. As soon as he was through the gate, he whipped his tail straight up in the air and charged over to his favorite spot to roll. That was the way he scratched the itches on his back. He always went for this one place in the field where the ground was bare and got himself all covered with dirt. What a sight he was. When the ground was muddy, like it was today, Sugar turned so brown, he looked like he was dipped in chocolate.

I went back inside the barn and raked the floor of the stall. Then I filled up the wheelbarrow and pushed it outside to the manure pile. I was huffing and puffing all the way along the path because the load was really heavy and I was trying to go as fast as I could. Sometimes I wish I had a brother or a sister to help with the chores. But my parents decided they didn't want any more children after they had me. My mom says I'm lucky to be the only child in the family. She has an older brother, and they used to fight when they were kids. He's my uncle Max. He and my mom grew up on our farm when it belonged to their parents. They died before I was born. My mom and dad kept the farm, and Uncle Max decided to live in town. He thought farming was too hard, so he moved into Riverview. He owns the barbershop on Main Street, but he doesn't work much anymore. He retired last year. Even though he's pretty old, Uncle Max can still ride horses and do all kinds of neat things.

This morning Uncle Max was going to teach me and Sugar how to jump over a fence. That was why I was in a hurry. I still had to brush Sugar and get him saddled before Uncle Max came by for my lesson. The truth was that Sugar already knew how to jump because my mom trained him to show and all before I even knew how to ride. People called Sugar "the dancing horse" because of the way he pranced around with my mom on his back. They were beautiful to watch together—it was just like they *were* dancing. My mom and Sugar even won a blue ribbon one year at the county fair. You might remember that stuff my dad said about me wanting a new saddle for the horse shows. Well, that really wasn't true at all. I don't know why my dad said that. He knows I'm never going to enter Sugar in a horse show, at least not as long as that show-off, Cynthia Anderson, and her snobby friends are around.

I just can't stand the way Cynthia always makes such a big deal out of it. I mean it's only a horse show. Cynthia is going into fifth grade like Emily and I are. Only Cynthia lives in town. She boards her horse, Tarzan, at her father's stable, and she enters all the shows and almost always wins. It's not that Tarzan isn't a great horse—I'm not saying that —but the way Cynthia brags about him all the time. You'd think her horse was God's gift or something. Cynthia gets Tarzan a new saddle practically every year, and she wears a different riding outfit to every single show. I told Emily I'd rather not enter shows than parade around like Cynthia Anderson does.

Anyway, I had more fun riding trails through the woods around our house, and training with Uncle Max on the cavalletti course. By the time I saddled Sugar and brought him down to the lower field, Uncle Max was already there, moving around the little cavalletti rails. Every rail was an obstacle that Sugar and I would ride over. Uncle Max had on his big old cowboy boots, and he was stepping off the distance between the rails. He placed them down a different way for each lesson. Today he made one long zigzag that led right up to a two-rail fence. When Uncle Max turned in my direction, I saw the funny-looking corncob pipe he always had in his mouth. He'd quit smoking his pipe a long time ago, but he still liked to chew on it.

I watched as Uncle Max pulled off the top rail of the fence so that Sugar and I would have to jump only the bottom rail. That was going to be our last obstacle; and even though I knew it would be only a couple of feet off the ground, I was still pretty nervous about it. Sugar could do the jump easily. There was no doubt about that. With my mom riding him, he even made it over the top rail. But I hadn't jumped him all that much, so I didn't know if Sugar trusted me enough yet to jump over the fence.

When Uncle Max saw me, he yelled, "How's our Rosie today, eh?"

"I'm okay, Uncle Max." I waved at him and walked Sugar over to the fence at the side of the field. Then I put on my safety helmet. My mom made me wear one. I didn't really need to, but wearing it saved her from worrying about me falling and getting a concussion. I didn't like the feel of the strap under my chin, so I pushed it up under the helmet with my hair. Sugar whinnied and told me to hurry up. To mount him, I usually lower one of the stirrups so I can reach it with my foot, and then jump up and over the saddle. It's kind of tricky for me because I'm so short. If I'm feeling lazy or if I'm in a rush, I cheat and climb a fence next to Sugar, and then I just hop over onto his back. Uncle Max teased me today when he saw me mounting up that way.

"Rosie," he said, "I'm gonna bring along a stepladder for you one of these days."

But I was already in the saddle. I just laughed and patted Sugar on the neck. "You see, Uncle Max," I said. "I don't need a ladder."

From somewhere behind me I heard my mom's voice

calling all of a sudden. "Max," she yelled, "it'll have to be a short lesson today. Rosie and I have to go into town this afternoon to do our shopping."

Uncle Max took his pipe out of his mouth, and then he yelled back to my mom, "Right you are, Maggie. We're just gonna hop a few rails, and one little fence."

I turned around to see where my mom was. She was standing about ten feet away from me, and as soon as she saw the mud on my face and the front of my shirt, she said, "A bath for you, young lady, or you're not going with me anywhere."

"Okay, okay, Mom," I told her, "I'll take another bath right after my lesson." She shook her head and started back across the grass toward the house.

It wasn't like my mom was really upset with me or anything. She knew I always got dirty brushing Sugar. The mud from Sugar's mane and back splattered all over and even got in my hair. There was no way not to get dirty, and I took more baths than anybody I knew.

Uncle Max teased me again, hollering over his shoulder, "Is our bathing beauty ready to ride?"

The sun was all the way up now, and it made the wet grass sparkle out in front of me. I walked Sugar to the start of the course, where Uncle Max was waiting. He grabbed Sugar's bridle and held him steady from the side, saying, "Now, I just want you to remember what I told you, Rosie.

Keep up the pace across the rails and help Sugar find his way to the fence. Remember, he has a blind spot in front, and he can't see what he's jumping over too well. So you have to be his eyes."

Uncle Max had already explained to me that horses don't see the way people do. Since a horse has eyes on the sides of his head, he can't really see some things right in front of him. So before the jumps, Sugar might not be able to tell exactly how high the rails and the fence are. He'd have to trust me to help him. I tightened my grip on the reins a little, then clucked my tongue. Sugar knew right where to go. He trotted toward the first rail at a pretty good pace while I posted up and down on the saddle. When Sugar got going faster, my rear end barely even touched down, and my stomach kept jiggling up and down like crazy inside.

My uncle shouted to me, "Make him dance, Rosie. Make him dance!"

Uncle Max said "dance" because of the way Sugar lifted his front legs over the rails. He looked like he was dancing. There were six rails to cross before the fence rail, and Sugar went over them like they weren't even there. After the last rail, there was a short canter to the fence. Uncle Max yelled something to me, but I couldn't hear what he was saying. That fence was getting closer and closer. For a second I thought Sugar was going to go crashing right through it. But then, all of a sudden, we flew up in the air, and I just held my breath.

My stomach was still flying up in the air as we came down on the other side of the fence. Sugar had his ears back when we hit the ground again. Just as we landed, my safety helmet popped off my head and my hair fell down into my face. You see, I have all this thick red hair that's always getting tangled, so it was like I had a scarf covering my eyes. I could hardly see where we were going.

Uncle Max shouted, "Bring him around, Rosie."

At the sound of my uncle's voice, Sugar turned so quickly that I lost my balance and fell forward on the saddle. Somehow the reins slipped out of my hands, and so I grabbed Sugar's mane and held on as tight as I could. I thought Sugar might take off and gallop across the field. But he must have known something was wrong because he slowed up right away and trotted straight back to Uncle Max.

Boy, was I embarrassed. My face must have turned about a hundred shades of red. Uncle Max was chuckling away, like I was the funniest rider he ever saw. He asked, "Are you all right, Rosie?"

"I guess so," I said, pulling the hair out of my eyes.

Uncle Max grabbed the reins and looked up at me. His face wrinkled into a big smile.

He said, "That wasn't too bad at all. Next time,

though, we'll make sure that helmet stays on your head, won't we? And we'll pay more attention to your posture. It's like dancing, Rosie."

"What do you mean, Uncle Max?" I asked.

"Well," he said, "you try to look graceful when you dance, don't you?"

I nodded that I did try, and Uncle Max said, "Graceful is how you ought to look when you ride. Think about your posture in that saddle when you're moving with Sugar. As you find his rhythm, you want to have a little bit more play in your spine. You know what I mean?"

"You mean I'm too stiff?" I asked.

Uncle Max chewed on his pipe for a second. Then he said, "You want to use the muscles in your back just like Sugar does when he jumps. Watch how he arches his back the next time your mom takes him out. He gathers everything in and then just lets it all out when he gets to the fence. And watch how your mom goes with him into the jump, how she stays up with him all the way through."

I slid down off my horse. Uncle Max was still holding the reins. "There you go," he said, handing them back to me, "what do you say we put on your helmet and try it again."

The next time my jumps were a lot smoother, and my helmet stayed on my head. It was almost like Sugar was dancing with me the way he did with my mom! Afterward,

Uncle Max said he'd walk Sugar to cool him off and then put him back in his stall. He told me to hurry along into the house. I had to get myself ready to go with my mom into town to buy my toe shoes and find a present for Sugar. I gave Uncle Max a great big hug good-bye and I whispered to him not to say anything to Sugar about his birthday tomorrow. I was pretty sure Sugar wouldn't remember it was his birthday, and I wanted it to be a surprise.

Chapter 3

An hour later my mom drove me into Riverview. We live pretty close to town, so the whole trip took only about fifteen minutes. Riverview is a tiny town. People who live around here say that if you blink your eyes driving through, you'll miss most of the town. On Main Street there's only my uncle's barber shop, the supermarket, the bank, the post office, a few little stores, and one blinking yellow traffic light. The dancewear store and the tack shop are in a shopping center that's a couple of miles past the center of town. That's where we were going.

The car windows were open, and I leaned my head out far enough to feel the breeze on my face. It was so hot, my blouse was sticking to the back of my seat. My mom and I didn't really talk while we were in the car. She didn't like to talk too much when she was driving. I was just sort of looking out the window and wondering to myself again what to get Sugar for his birthday. That new saddle was totally out of the question unless I put off getting my toe shoes. What if I broke that deal I'd made with my mom and didn't get shoes? The more I tried not to think about it, the more I thought about it. There was one thing I knew for sure: if I didn't get toe shoes, I'd never be a ballerina.

My mom looked over at me and asked, "Is your seat belt fastened, Rosie?"

"Sure it is," I told her. She must have asked about my seat belt thirty or forty times every time she drove me anywhere in the car.

As we turned on the road that led into town, I stared up at the tree branches that were flying by overhead. The sun was playing hide-and-seek behind the leaves. All of a sudden I heard a dog barking at us from the side of the road. We were passing by Uncle Max's house, and the dog barking was Sherlock's sister, Shirley. They looked so much alike, you could hardly tell them apart even though they were boy and girl bloodhounds. Seeing Shirley there on the road made me think of Sherlock and what that crazy dog had done to Sugar's brush. I started to get mad at him all over again, but then I got this great idea.

The brush that Sherlock ruined was the kind called a dandy brush, and Sugar sure did need a new one now. That could be the perfect present! When we pulled into the shopping center, I told my mom, "I think I figured out what to get Sugar for his birthday so he won't feel too bad about having to wait for a new saddle."

"What's that, dear?"

"I'll get him a dandy brush to replace the one that Sherlock chewed up this morning. And I'll tell Sugar that he gets to have me brush him at least once a day with his new brush for the whole year."

"That sounds like a good idea. Sugar loves to be brushed. We'll stop in the tack shop later. But first, let's go into Gleason's and find your toe shoes."

Gleason's Dancewear was the only place around that sold toe shoes. They also sold leotards and tights and leg warmers and stuff like that. But it was still a tiny store, about the size you might expect to find in a tiny town like ours. Once my mom and I were inside, a saleslady used a tape to measure my two feet. While we were waiting for the woman to bring out a pair of shoes for me to try on, my mom said to me, "When we get home, I'll show you how to wax your shoes, so they'll hold up longer."

"Are you kidding?" I said. "You put wax on toe shoes?"

"That's right," said my mom. "Floor wax just like I use on the kitchen floor. The wax dries hard. It protects the shoes and makes them last."

The saleslady came back with a pair of toe shoes for

me to try. I loved the shiny pink satin and the really sleek shape of the shoes. But I was hardly able to squeeze my feet into them! "I think these are way to small," I told her.

While I stood up in the shoes, the woman knelt down to feel where my toes were. She was a nice enough lady, but she sort of ignored me and spoke to my mom. "I'm sure these are a proper fit for your daughter. They have to be tight enough to support her feet when she goes up on pointe."

"Tight!" I said. "It feels like my feet are stuck inside of two little thimbles."

But neither my mom nor the saleslady said anything to me. They just looked at each other and smiled.

Then Mrs. Gleason came up from behind me, and she spoke to my mom too, so it was like I had just disappeared. Mrs. Gleason said, real excited, "Oh, they're gorgeous, Mrs. Daniels, and we do like them snug." For some reason, I never liked that word, *gorgeous,* when the person saying it was all worked up the way Mrs. Gleason was. It sounded kind of phony.

My mom told me that she'd heard Mrs. Gleason used to be a ballerina. But I didn't believe it because Mrs. Gleason was so heavy on her feet the way she moved and all. It wasn't like she was graceful or anything. Plus she had these two little hairs on her lip that looked pretty funny. She patted me on the head and said she thought I would be

a lovely little dancer. That really got to me. Boy, oh, boy— lovely *little* dancer. How would she know what kind of dancer I was? I didn't say anything, though. I shrugged my shoulders and tried my best to smile.

My mom and I left the store with four pairs of toe shoes in a shopping bag that I carried under my arm. We also bought some pink ribbons that my mom said she would show me how to sew on the shoes after we got home. But I was already positive they were going to be a disaster. I mean, how was I ever going to get up on pointe with all the blood squeezed out of my feet? A total disaster! But my mom insisted toe shoes had to fit just the way those ladies in the store said. "You'll see, Rosie," she said. "Toe shoes always feel awkward and tight at first on everyone. But you'll get used to them."

I hoped my mom was right. We'd spent nearly two hundred dollars. That was a whole lot more than all the money from my piggy bank. But I'd kept twenty dollars to buy Sugar a brush.

The tack shop was just a short walk through the shopping center parking lot. The name of the store was Anderson's Horse and Buggy Shop. It was owned by Cynthia Anderson's father, who also owned the biggest stable anywhere around. Mr. Anderson sold all kinds of things for horses—saddles, blankets, bridles, and tons of riding outfits. And horse brushes, of course. He didn't sell buggies, but he kept this old one on display in front of the store. It was over a hundred years old, so nobody ever used it. But Mr. Anderson let my mom and me climb inside and sit on the leather seat. That was fun, because I made believe Sugar was taking us on a long trip through the mountains.

My dad once said Mr. Anderson made a killing every year on the tourists who stayed at the ski lodges that were out near his stables. A lot of those skiers liked to rent Mr. Anderson's horses and go riding in the woods around the ski slopes. Except during hunting season, because there were too many hunters in the woods. If you were crazy enough to go horseback riding then, you or your horse might just get shot by mistake! I never rode Sugar anywhere near the woods when the hunters were there. Even where we lived, sometimes you could hear their gunshots coming from close by.

Mr. Anderson was a hunter, and he'd shot a black bear and then stuffed its head. It was on a wall behind the counter in the tack shop. The bear's eyeballs were looking right at me when my mom and I went over to the counter to find a dandy brush. The eyes were sort of creepy the way they followed me everywhere I went. It was almost like he was still alive up there, and he looked mad. I asked my mom where the rest of the bear's body was, but she didn't know.

Mr. Anderson must have heard us from behind the

counter. He laughed and said, "The rest of that bear's gone to meet his maker, Rosie. He's roaming around up in bear heaven."

I asked him, "How can he be roaming around anywhere without his head?"

He laughed, and my mom said, "Show Mr. Anderson which brush you want, Rosie."

I pointed it out to him and said, "That one in the back with the little gold horseshoe painted on it." While Mr. Anderson was putting the brush in a box, I told my mom, "The horseshoe will be good luck for Sugar."

Mr. Anderson handed the box to me and said, "It seems to me Sugar's already a mighty lucky horse."

"What do you mean?" I asked him.

He smiled at me, and then he said, "Sugar has *you* riding him and taking care of him, doesn't he? Not only that. He has four horseshoes on his feet. So Sugar's got to be at least four times as lucky as any of us people."

Just then Cynthia walked into the store, and so I wasn't feeling too lucky myself. Cynthia was the last person I wanted to see. She pranced over and gave her father a kiss on the cheek. Then she said, "Hello, Rosie. I see somebody's getting ready for Miss Bradley's pointe class. Or are you riding Sugar in toe shoes these days?"

"Very funny, Cynthia." She was in my ballet class too. But Cynthia wasn't too hot in ballet. She was the prettiest girl in our class, with all of this blond hair and a beautiful face. But she never really worked very hard as far as I could see, and Miss Bradley was on her case all the time.

"Well, we'd better get going, Mom," I said. "Thanks again, Mr. Anderson. See ya, Cynthia."

I tried to nudge my mom's elbow to get us to leave, but the bag of toe shoes fell out of my arms, spilling the shoes out onto the floor at my feet. I could hardly believe what happened then. Cynthia Anderson actually bent down and helped me pick up my shoes. Why was she being so nice all of a sudden? I didn't trust her for a second.

Cynthia picked up one of the shoes and said, "You take the same size as me, Rosie. And look, we even have the same maker for our shoes."

"How do you know?" I asked her.

Cynthia held the pink shoe up under my nose and pointed to a little diamond that was stamped on the sole of the shoe. "You see that mark," she said, sounding like Little Miss Know-It-All. "Every shoemaker has a special mark, and ours is that diamond. Didn't you know that?"

Then I remembered Mrs. Gleason explaining that every pair of pointe shoes has to be made by hand, and that every shoemaker has a different sign or letter that got stamped on the bottom of the shoe. I told Cynthia, "Oh, yeah, I know about that diamond. I just forgot for a second."

I felt so dumb and my face got really hot all of a sudden. Cynthia always made me feel that way. She was nasty even if she pretended to be nice. That was just the way she was. But I thanked her anyway. Just as my mom and I were leaving the tack shop, I looked back over the counter, and there was that bear staring at me again. He really was. No kidding. Only now, from where I was, he looked like he was up there grinning at me. I practically ran out the door.

I told my mom when we got back in the car, "That Cynthia Anderson really gives me the creeps."

My mom said, "Cynthia seemed very sweet. You both ride and take ballet. I don't see why the two of you aren't better friends. You have a lot in common. You're not jealous of her, are you, Rosie?"

"No way!" I said. "You don't know her, Mom. You should see the way she and her friends act in school. Or in ballet class. Just ask Emily. Cynthia always makes fun of her because Emily wears glasses and has braces on her teeth."

My mom didn't say anything else about Cynthia. On our way home we stopped at the drugstore in town and picked up wrapping paper and ribbon for Sugar's present. When we finally drove into the driveway of our farm, I saw my dad on the tractor out in back of the barn. The tractor was already fixed, and he was plowing over the dirt so it would be ready to plant next year.

My mom honked the horn a couple times, and my dad waved to us. Then my mom parked the car out in front of the garage. She said, "Take your toe shoes into the garage. That's where we'll wax them so the fumes don't get in the house."

"Okay, Mom," I said. "But first I want to take them into the barn to show Sugar."

"Oh, Rosalie," said my mom. She sounded tired. As I went running off with the bag of toe shoes, I heard her yell after me, "Meet me in the garage in five minutes, do you hear?"

"Okay, I will," I hollered over my shoulder. Sugar stayed in the stall on most afternoons when the weather was hot like it was today. It was the beginning of September, and he was already getting his thick winter coat. So he had to stay inside, where it was shady and cooler for him. When I went into the barn, I found him taking a nap, leaning up against the wall of his stall. His eyes were closed. He was sleeping and standing up at the same time, and swishing away flies with his tail.

As soon as he heard me at the door to his stall, he popped open his big eyes and yawned like he was saying hello. I put my hands inside a pair of toe shoes and held them up in front of his nose. Sugar put his ears back and sniffed the shoes to make sure that they weren't carrots. Then he neighed and shook his head up and down like he was saying "Wow!" He did that again after I made my toe shoes tap-dance over the top of the wooden door in front of his stall. He was happy for me.

Before I went to meet my mom, I whispered in Sugar's ear, "Someday, Sugar, you can come and watch me dance on a great big stage. Won't that be fun for you?"

He shook his head again, and I showed him how Miss Bradley taught us to bow for an audience. She said it was important to let the audience see your heart. I wasn't really sure what she meant by that, so for Sugar, I just curtsied, and made believe that I was telling him good-bye and saying that I loved him with all my heart. Then I ran out of the barn and skipped along the driveway to the garage.

My mom was sure right about the fumes from that floor wax. We both just about suffocated in the garage while she showed me how to put the wax on my shoes with a toothbrush. When we were finished, I asked her, "Are we always going to have to do this, I mean, for all of my pointe shoes?"

She said, "That's right, kiddo. So you better get used to it. We may want to darn them later with some thread around the toes. We'll wait and see how they turn out."

After dinner my mom showed me where to sew the

ribbons on the sides of the shoes. She told me that tomorrow we'd have to pound the toes with a hammer to make them softer and quieter on the floor. I told her, "It seems like an awful lot of trouble you have to go through just to dance."

My mom said, "You always get back what you put into things, Rosie. So it's worth it in the long run. You'll see."

"I guess so," I said, but I really wasn't sure. How long was the long run anyway?

Before I got ready for bed, I wrapped up Sugar's brush and tied a bow on it. I still had to make a card for him, but my dad poked his head into my bedroom and told me, "It's ten o'clock and it's way past your bedtime, Rosie." If there's one thing I can't stand, it's going to bed before I'm sleepy. I keep my flashlight on the night table so that I can read under the covers if I can't get to sleep. After I put on my pajamas and said good night to my mom and dad, I turned out the light and took my diary under the covers with me.

All of a sudden I was inside a dark cave with a flashlight and my pen. One time, I got ink from my pen on the sheets, and my mom got pretty angry with me. So tonight I was extra careful and wrote a little poem for Sugar in my diary. Tomorrow morning I'd have to rewrite it on the birthday card that I was going to give him with his present.

Dear Sugar,
I know you'll understand,
   because you always do,
That I still can't afford
   a new saddle for you.

But I thought of a way
   to make that all right,
By finding a reason for us
   to visit at night.

I'll say, "Mommy and Daddy,
   I'm in such a rush,
I forgot to give Sugar
   his once-a-day brush!"

So now you know
   and soon you will see
This dandy new brush
   I've brought with me.

It will get out most tangles
   with one gentle touch,
Oh, Sugar, it really is
   just too much!

The wrapping paper's full
   of hearts just for you,

And I hope you don't mind
   that the ribbon's not blue.

I've surely not forgotten
   that you are a male,
But the store in town had
   a pink-ribbon sale.

Now we know what's inside,
   so it's no mystery,
But let's open the box
   and see what we see.

I was just finishing it when I heard my mom's voice at my door. She said, "Lights out in there, Rosie. That means your flashlight too." I turned off the flashlight and curled up in my bed. Even with my head on my pillow I could see the sky outside my window and millions of stars twinkling like crazy. They were in heaven, and that was where luck came from. Before I fell off to sleep, I said my prayers to myself and hoped the horseshoe on Sugar's new brush was going to bring him lots and lots of good luck.

Chapter 4

Sunday morning was so cold I had to wear a jacket when I went outside. It was only around fifty degrees, and my dad said he was worried that we might get an early frost this year. That would be bad for our fruit trees and the crops on our farm that hadn't been harvested yet. We had lots of apple trees and pear trees. Plus all kinds of vegetables. If the weather turned colder, then my dad would have to put smoke pots out in the fields. They were these pots that burned kerosene to keep the trees and plants warm at night. When the pots were burning, they made big clouds of smelly smoke. It was really putrid. One time my mom told me not to breathe in the smoke because it would stunt my growth and then I'd be short forever. So when I walked out to the barn to give Sugar his birthday brush, I looked straight up in the sky and hoped that gold horseshoe on the brush would bring lucky weather too.

I better tell you, there was this one other reason I was hoping for lucky weather. My mom said at breakfast that if it stayed nice, I could ride Sugar all the way to town for my ballet class on Monday afternoon. She said I could ride just as long as we took the back way to town and stayed off the roads, where there were too many cars. I was pretty excited and looking forward to tomorrow. But at the very same time, I was getting more and more worried about that class, because I'd be going on pointe for the first time and all. What if I fell down in front of everybody? I knew Cynthia Anderson would never let me hear the end of it.

The chill in the air sure did make Sugar frisky. When I put him in the back field, he galloped around and around in circles like he was chasing after his tail. Then he bucked and jumped up in the air like he was dancing a jig and kicking his heels. I yelled to him, "Yippie ay yay! Yahoo! Hip, hip, hooray and happy birthday to you!" Then I held out one hand in his direction and crinkled the cellophane wrapper from a piece of candy that I was holding in my other hand. It was a red and white Starlight Mint, which was Sugar's most favorite candy in the whole world. Uncle Max taught me this trick with the wrapper. Sugar heard it from far away and he came racing over to where I was standing in about two seconds flat. He put his head over the top of the fence, and I let him lick that mint out of the palm of my hand with his wet tongue. Sugar's tongue tickled like crazy, and it made my hand sort of gooey, but it was worth it anyhow.

My dad used to say that horses were "really dumb." He meant that they weren't as smart as dogs or cats. But I made my dad a bet. I bet him a dollar Sugar would come running only for Starlight Mints, and no other kind of candy. So my dad tried to call Sugar by crinkling up wrappers from just about every kind of candy he could think of. But Sugar could tell the difference every single time, and he just ignored my dad, except when it was a Starlight Mint. Honest, my dad tried everything. He finally paid me the dollar he owed me and said he guessed horses were a lot smarter than he ever thought. Of course, Sugar and I knew that all along.

While I brushed Sugar down with his new brush, I kept checking the sky for rain clouds. I didn't see any, but the weather can change really fast around here. I told Sugar, "It better not rain tomorrow, or we won't be able to ride into town together. Mom will want to drive me instead." Just when I said that, I felt the first raindrop on my cheek, and sure enough when I looked up again, there was this one tiny little gray cloud over my head. I hurried to get Sugar back to the barn. When we went inside, my mom was there. She was putting away some bottles of apple jelly and strawberry jam which she made herself and kept in a little room in the barn. She was always putting stuff like that in bottles and storing them so we'd have lots to eat all winter.

After I put Sugar back in his stall, I helped my mom put her bottles on shelves in the storage room. She said, "One of these days, Rosie, I'm going to teach you how to do this. I was about your age, eleven or twelve, I think, when my mother first taught me how to put away preserves. Who knows? Someday you may want to teach your children—"

Her voice just sort of stopped before she'd even finished what she was saying. I said, "Oh, Mom, how can I possibly know if I'm ever gonna have children when I grow up? I'm too young to think about all that stuff."

My mom just laughed and put the last bottle on the shelf. She was always talking about me growing up, and getting married, and having a family and all. And sometimes she'd tease me about it. But those kinds of things only made my head feel dizzy. One time I made my mom a bet I would never get married. But that was a pretty silly bet I made. I mean, sometimes I want to grow up, and other times I don't. Sometimes I like boys—they're okay once in a while—but lots of times they're really dumb, and then I don't like them one bit.

Like the first time Stephen Archer came to ballet class. Stephen and his folks live on a farm about a mile down the road from us. But they don't farm their farm. His parents just like living in a big farmhouse. I can't see what good it is having a farm and not growing anything. They don't even plant a garden or keep any animals. Anyway, last year Stephen's mom made him start taking ballet. Stephen's really into sports—he plays baseball and football in school—and so he didn't want to dance much at all. Stephen tried to get out of going to Miss Bradley's class by bringing this little garter snake with him the first time he came to her studio.

Boy, was he in for a surprise. He thought Miss Bradley was sure to throw him out of class if he let that garter snake loose on the floor and scared all of us. But when Miss Bradley saw the snake slithering around in the studio, she walked right over and picked it up from behind its head. Then she just went outside and let it go free. She didn't even say anything about it at first. Later, though, she told us that she grew up in the country with a brother who acted dumb like Stephen, and so she wasn't afraid of snakes.

I'm not afraid of snakes either except when I'm riding, because Sugar can get spooked by a snake if he comes up on one by surprise. That's just what happened on Monday when I rode him to my ballet class. The weather turned out to be nice so my mom said I could ride to town. My class was at one o'clock, and so we had to go before noon to make it on time and all. I was planning to leave Sugar with my uncle at his barber shop while I was in my pointe class. The ballet studio was only a short walk around the corner from the barber shop, and I knew Uncle Max would be happy to take care of Sugar. So I put my toe shoes in a saddlebag with the rest of my dance stuff and headed out to the barn.

Just as Sugar and I were starting off, my mom came out of the house and yelled to me, "Don't forget to buckle that helmet, young lady."

I lifted my chin and showed her it was buckled. My mom was always worrying about me falling off my horse because that's what happened to her when she was a girl. She broke her ankle and had to quit dancing because it never healed right. She didn't talk about it much, but I knew my mom was afraid the same thing might happen to me. When Sugar and I reached the end of our driveway, my mom yelled after me, "Rosalie, remember what I told you about riding on Main Street. You walk him at the side of the street. Do you hear me?"

"Okay, okay, Mom," I said. But we almost never made it to Main Street anyway!

Sugar and I started off on Mountain Valley Road. That's the road we live on. There aren't many houses, and we stayed by the curb on the grass, where a sidewalk would have been if there had been any sidewalks. Once we had gone as far as the Archers' farmhouse, we took the Rain Man Trail. It's an old Indian trail through the forest, and you could find arrowheads buried there if you looked hard enough. I was taught in school last year that we should say Native American instead of Indian. But lots of times I forget. My fourth-grade teacher, Mrs. Gilroy, said we should say *Native Americans* because the Indians lived in America way before our ancestors came here, and that made them natives.

It's funny, the things you remember even when you don't decide to or anything. When Sugar and I were on that Rain Man Trail, I was thinking of that stuff Mrs. Gilroy taught us about Native Americans. And I was wondering why it was we didn't call Indians who lived in India *Native Indians*. And then I asked myself, what about an American Indian who was living in India? Was he still a native? I liked that word, *native,* just the way it sort of made my tongue go up and down real fast when I said it.

I could think about things like that and keep my eye on the trail at the same time. I had to watch out for holes that Sugar might step into, and I always had to keep looking out for tree branches in our path that might poke out one of his eyes or one of mine. If you thought about things too hard and you didn't watch the trail, sooner or later you'd get whipped in the face by a branch. That happened to me a few times on the Rain Man Trail. But Sugar helped because he already knew the whole trail, and he was always looking for the easiest way for us to go. A lot of the time I just let the reins loose and let him lead the way. I did that even though you're really not supposed to ever let your horse decide where you're going.

But today I just felt like letting Sugar decide. Even when we came to the fork in the trail about halfway into town, I asked Sugar which way he wanted to go: along the path by the river, or the way that went through the clearing where the Rain Men used to dance for rain? Sugar went toward the clearing.

It was at the top of a hill mostly surrounded by pine trees. I don't know why the Rain Men chose this exact spot to do their dancing. But it might have been because both rain and luck came from heaven, and this place was about the highest ground in the forest. So I guess it was about as close as you could get to heaven around here. Sugar liked to eat the tall grass in that clearing because it was so sweet. There were millions of pine needles and pine cones and even some crab apples lying on the ground too. So when we got up there, Sugar just had to stop for a snack.

That was when we saw the snake. Only this one was no puny little garter snake. It was a big old black snake, and I don't know which of us saw it first. It was coming

through the grass toward us, and it stopped right in front of Sugar and lifted up its head and stuck out its tongue real fast. The next thing I knew, I was flying through the air. Sugar ran right out from under me, he was so scared and all. I came down in a gully that was full of water, and I landed hard on my rear end with a big splash. I don't know where that black snake went. It was probably scared, too, and ran away to hide in the grass. When I looked around, I couldn't even see where Sugar had gone.

But I heard him from behind me. He screamed twice like he was saying, "Rosie! Where are you?"

I yelled, "Sugar! Come back. I'm down here."

I was lucky that I was wearing my safety helmet, because I banged up the back of my head when I went down in that gulley. When I got to my feet and climbed out of there, Sugar was nowhere to be seen. I was really scared all of a sudden because I wasn't sure I could catch him out here in the middle of nowhere. I said to myself, "It was just a dumb old snake, Sugar. You didn't have to go all the way to Mars, you know." Then I saw him standing by the edge of the trees all the way across the clearing.

I started walking over toward him real slow so he wouldn't get spooked again by mistake. If he ran into the woods, I'd have a really hard time catching up with him. But at least he looked like he wasn't hurt or anything. When I was about ten or fifteen feet away from him, I just stopped and then waited to see what he was going to do. He was looking straight at me, and he lowered his head down, like he was sort of embarrassed.

Then all of a sudden he started toward me, and he came all the way to me and gave me his reins. "Oh, Sugar," I whispered to him, and I don't know why, but I just started crying while I went around him and lowered the stirrup so I could mount up again. That horse stood as still as he could to try to help. My rear end was soaking wet, and it sure hurt like the dickens after I finally got back up on the saddle. I was wearing my dance tights underneath my blue jeans, and I could tell they were both soaked through and through. And we still had a long way to go before we'd reach Riverview.

But how could I go to class with wet tights? I was really in for it now. My tights were sure to look like I had an accident in them. And if Miss Bradley didn't let me take pointe class, everyone in school would know about it tomorrow, because tomorrow was the first day of school.

I was a total wreck when Sugar and I finally got to Main Street. I tried to hide behind him while we were walking so no one would see me. At my uncle's barbershop I tied Sugar to the barber pole on the porch outside. It was this red, white, and blue striped pole that looked like a big candy cane. Uncle Max said it was a real antique. Anyway,

I ran into the shop with tears streaming down my cheeks and all. Uncle Max said, "Hey there! You'd better slow down, little lady."

The screen door slammed behind me, and I practically fell down over Uncle Max's big boots. He was sitting in a chair by the door, and he got up fast. Then he picked me right up in his arms and laughed his funny laugh. He sounded almost like a foghorn. He said, "What in the world has happened to you, Rosie? Feels like you wet your pants."

"Oh, Uncle Max. There was a snake, and Sugar ran away, and I fell in the water, and now I'm late for ballet class and my tights are all wet." I was sort of crying and running out of breath at the same time. There was one old barber named Hank who was cutting a man's hair. I could see the two of them staring at me and Uncle Max, but I didn't care, because it wasn't their business anyway. I was still sobbing pretty hard. I said to Uncle Max, "What am I gonna do now? Oh, what am I gonna do, Uncle Max? I can't go to class like this!"

He said, "You take yourself into the back room there, Rosie, and get out of those wet britches. When you get them off, hand them out the door to me. No need for any more tears. We'll get you fixed up in no time." Uncle Max handed me a towel to wrap around my waist, and I did exactly what he told me to do. The clock on the wall said twelve-thirty, and so I had only half an hour to get to class. After I went inside that little room and took off my blue jeans and my soggy tights, I handed them out from behind the door. Then I poked my head out to see what Uncle Max was going to do.

Chapter 5

$\mathcal{P}$eeking through the doorway, I watched Uncle Max sit down in one of the big barber chairs. He swiveled it around and said to the barber named Hank, "Hand me that blow dryer, old buddy."

Hank gave my uncle the hair dryer, and Uncle Max held up my wet tights and started drying them with the hot air. Then he did the same with my jeans and my undies and even my sneakers. After about twenty minutes, everything was dry again. You could hardly even see the stain on my tights. When he handed my clothes back, I said, "Gee, thanks, Uncle Max. You're the best unc—"

But he didn't let me finish. He said, "Oh, go on, Rosie. If you hang around here gabbing all day, you'll be late for that dance class of yours. Now you skidaddle, and don't worry about Sugar. I may just give him a haircut while you're gone. That mane of his could use a trim."

I put my clothes back on and ran outside to let Sugar know I was okay. Then I took the saddlebags with me and ran all the way from the barbershop to Miss Bradley's dance studio. It was inside this little red brick building that used to be a one-room schoolhouse. My mom and Uncle Max both went to school there when they were kids, and that was way before the school that I go to had even been built.

Miss Bradley had taped up a sign on the glass of the front door, and it said THIS IS STRICTLY A BALLET STUDIO. I DO NOT OFFER TAP, JAZZ, OR BALLROOM DANCING. BEGINNER AND IN-TERMEDIATE CLASSES AVAILABLE. PLEASE TAKE OFF YOUR SHOES.

Miss Bradley made up this rule that you couldn't wear your shoes in the studio. You had to take them off at the front door, like people do over in Japan, and then you put on a pair of these fluffy pink or blue slippers that Miss Bradley kept in a rack out by the door. Some of the parents who came into the studio really didn't like having to take their shoes off and all. Like my dad. He always just waited around for me outside whenever he came to pick me up from class.

Anyway, this afternoon I took off my sneakers and put on my own pair of black ballet slippers. Then I hurried down the hall. When I got to the dressing room, I was so nervous I could feel my heart pounding in my chest. I rushed right inside because I had only about two minutes to change. Miss Bradley didn't make us wear uniforms like some other teachers do. She just said that since we were each different on the inside, there was no need for us to look the same on the outside. Miss Bradley did say that we should always be neat and not try to hide our bodies with clothes that were too baggy. Up until Miss Bradley came to Riverview two years ago, I used to take class from Mrs. Grant. She made us all wear pink tights and pink leotards. But then Mrs. Grant moved out of town somewhere, and Miss Bradley took over running the studio and changed the rules.

Another one of her rules was that if you were late, then you weren't allowed to take class that day. So I was in really big trouble if I got there late for my first pointe class. That was what my heart was telling me and why my stomach was sort of doing flip-flops. I was the last person to get to the dressing room, and just as I was going in, Cynthia Anderson and Deidre Larson passed me in the doorway on their way out. Cynthia stopped long enough to say, "Ya better hurry up. The teacher's little pet can't be late now, can she? We'll tell Miss Bradley you're on your way, Rosie."

"Don't do me any favors, Cynthia," I said. I guess I sounded a little nasty, but Cynthia was going on and on lately how I was the teacher's pet, and that really burned me up. She called me that just because I worked harder at dancing than she did, and once in a while Miss Bradley asked me to demonstrate a step for the rest of the class. Even when we were younger, Cynthia always used to call me names. Like Carrot-Head and Twinkle-Toes. For some reason that really got me mad, and we almost got into a fight in the school yard when we were in fourth grade. My mom once told me to remember sticks and stones could break my bones, but words could never hurt me. But I didn't believe that for a second. Those names Cynthia called me hurt a lot sometimes.

Of course, she never said anything in front of grownups, so I knew I'd be safe once I went in the studio. Then Cynthia would probably be too busy checking herself in the mirror to say anything else to me anyway. Only today, it turned out, there was no mirror! Miss Bradley had put curtains up over all the mirrors in the studio. I found that out when I rushed in and almost ran into Miss Bradley, who was just closing the door. She told me, "Slow down, Rosie. I hope you remembered to sign in outside."

"Oh, Miss Bradley, I forgot!" I said. "I didn't want to be late and miss class."

"Don't worry about it now," she told me. "Just make sure you sign in before you leave."

It was one o'clock on the dot. After I left the saddlebag with my pointe shoes at the side of the studio, I put some rosin on my slippers to keep them from slipping and sliding over the wood floor. There was a box of rosin in the corner that you scuffed and stamped your shoes in so the bottoms would be covered with rosin dust. One time I got dust in my eyes and practically had to leave class because I couldn't stop the tears from coming out of my eyes. So I was careful not to get any rosin on my hands. I found a place at one of the portable barres near the back of the room and got ready for the first exercise.

That was when I saw this big smirk on Cynthia's face. She was right next to me, but I just ignored her. Emily was on the other side of me. There were only ten girls taking class. Miss Bradley stood near the center of the floor and told us, "I'm doing us all a big favor today by not letting you watch yourselves. You may remember me telling you that ballet is a very special way we use our bodies to tell a story. That story must always come from our hearts, and that's why we practice all of these steps and positions in every class. Believe me, ladies, you'll never become ballerinas by staring in the mirror. You have to learn to see beyond that mirror so the audience can see with you."

I didn't know exactly what Miss Bradley meant, but I was pretty glad not to have to look at myself in the mirror because a lot of times I couldn't help comparing my body to the other girls like Cynthia and Deidre and Jennifer Taylor, and I really didn't feel too hot when I did that.

Sometimes I wanted to hide. I mean I'm so short, like I told you before, and I have these really, really long arms that go almost all the way to my knees. No kidding. My mom says that being pretty is just all in your head, but my head tells me I'm just never going to be pretty like those other girls.

I tried not to get down in the dumps about it, and I felt better once we started doing exercises at the barre. The music always made me happy. It was fun the way you had to try to keep ahead of the beat. The pianist, Mrs. Quill, always played for Miss Bradley's classes. She had long, shiny silver hair, and the fingers of her hands were real long. They looked like they were made out of ivory or something, just like the keys of the piano that she was playing.

Sometimes Miss Bradley got so excited that she just sang out loud over the music, and then she'd scream at us to tell us what we were doing wrong. No matter how well we did a step, it seemed like it was almost never good enough. But then it was fun when you finally got it right, or almost right. My favorite part of the class was right after the barre, when we did jumps across the floor. I was sure that I was the best jumper in the class. Even though I'm so short, I could still go higher in the air and farther across the floor than anybody else when I did a grande jeté.

If you don't know anything about ballet, then you

might not know all of the steps have these French names. Like plié, and tendu, and grande battement. I used to think the names sounded funny. But after Miss Bradley taught us what they meant and how we were supposed to do each of the steps, they didn't sound funny to me anymore. We always started the barre with pliés, which was where you sort of bent your knees and went down and up. But when you were going down, you were supposed to think of going up. And when you were going up, you were supposed to think that you were going down. Boy, was that ever confusing for me at first. One time Miss Bradley told me, "Try to resist the direction in which your body is moving, Rosie, and keep turning out your heart to the audience."

I liked that stuff about the heart and making believe that I was on a stage in front of an audience. But by the end of the barre exercises it was hard to make believe anything because I was so pooped. Miss Bradley told us it was time to put on our pointe shoes and try going up on our toes. I went over and grabbed my saddlebag and took out my shoes and ribbons. After I got them on and all, I saw Cynthia pointing down at my legs. She turned to Miss Bradley, and then said with this loud voice that sounded so phony, "Miss Bradley, are we supposed to tie our ribbons way up around our knees the way Rosie has them?" I looked down and saw that my ribbons came to the tops of my calves, where I had tied them in a bow. Cynthia laughed, and then she said, "Rosie looks like she has bowed legs and bows on her knees."

I started blushing, but Miss Bradley said to me in her soft voice, "You might lower those ribbons just a bit, Rosie, and tie them more neatly."

She showed me where to tie them above my ankles, and then we all took our places again at the barre. I looked at Cynthia, and she was smirking again. But now I was more worried about my toe shoes fitting so tight. Boy, they really hurt my feet even when I just walked slowly in them. I looked around at the other girls to see if their shoes hurt them too, like my mom said. But their faces were really just kind of blank and tense, and everybody looked awfully serious. I was holding my breath and squeezing the barre with both hands.

Miss Bradley said, "Now, I know your little feet must hurt in those brand-new shoes, but you'll break them in and get over that soon enough." None of us even dared say a word. It was really quiet. Then Miss Bradley cried out, "You all look like you're constipated. Relax and try breathing. Honestly, ladies. Those feet are not going to fall off. I promise you." After she said that, she screwed up her face and imitated the way we looked. Then it was like all of a sudden all of us just let out our breath and groaned and laughed at the same time.

I felt better after that. Miss Bradley said, "Now we're

going to roll up on pointe, and roll back down through the feet to the floor. I want you to start with your feet parallel in sixth position. Both hands close together on the barre. We're going to repeat this eight times. Don't forget those upper bodies of yours."

Miss Bradley asked Mrs. Quill to play something at a slow tempo, an adagio. Then all of us tried to go up on pointe, but it was an awful lot harder than it looked. I felt like an elephant was stepping on my toes. Miss Bradley told us not to hike up our shoulders and not to drop our chests, but how was I ever supposed to remember exactly what to do with every part of my body at the same time? Every time I fixed one part of me, some other part would go wrong. And my knees kept wanting to buckle under me every time I tried to go up on my toes.

Miss Bradley came around behind me and said, "Don't worry, Rosie. When your feet become more flexible, you'll be able to keep your knees straighter." Miss Bradley's eyes always seemed to sparkle when she talked. But what she said next made my heart go right into my throat. "I want everyone to watch Rosie show us how we roll down through the foot and reach all the way up to heaven at the same time. The rest of you are dropping onto your heels. Now, make a circle around Rosie."

All of a sudden everybody was looking at me, and I wished that I could turn invisible. Miss Bradley was

standing a few feet in front of me on the other side of the portable barre. She told me, "This time, Rosie, before you go up on your toes, I want you to think of someone you really love, and imagine them standing right here where I am. Okay? Just make believe for a minute you're Juliet reaching out for your Romeo. I want you to tell him how you feel with your heart. Say, 'I love you, Romeo.'"

I did what Miss Bradley said, but I thought of Sugar when I had to think of someone that I really loved. It took forever to get up on my toes, but reaching for Sugar somehow made it seem easier. I kept reaching for him even when I was going back down to the floor. When I was finished, I didn't know if I had done it right or not. But all of a sudden Miss Bradley yelled out, "Brava! That was beautiful, Rosie."

When she said that, my throat felt tight. I was so happy, I was afraid I might cry. I really had to look away when some of the other girls clapped. I was sort of happy and embarrassed at the same time. Afterward, in the dressing room, I got dressed as fast as I could and got my things together to leave. Emily asked me why I was in such a hurry, and I just told her I was late. Cynthia glared at me as I was going out the door with my saddlebag tucked under my arm. Just before I heard the door close, I heard her say to the other girls still inside, "There goes the teacher's pet." But I didn't care at all. I could hardly wait to get back and tell Sugar what happened in class.

He was waiting for me in front of the barbershop. And so was Uncle Max. I thanked Uncle Max again for drying my tights and for watching Sugar for me, and then Sugar and I started for home. While I was leading him down Main Street, Miss Bradley drove past us in her car and looked out the window at me for a second. She had kind of a funny expression on her face. But I waved to her and told Sugar, "That's Miss Bradley, my ballet teacher."

I was happy all day, even though I did keep wondering to myself about that weird look Miss Bradley had given me. Later that night, after I'd told my mom at the dinner table all about class, I went straight up to my room, and jumped up and down on my bed for a while. I guess I do get pretty excited sometimes. But I knew that Sugar would know just how I felt, and I wrote him another letter in my diary.

Dear Sugar,

It's a little hard explaining
    what I learned in class today,
You see, my ballet teacher taught me
    how to speak in a silent way.
She answered all these questions
    that were inside me all along;

Now I no longer have the feeling
    that I'm doing something wrong.
Sugar, there's certainly no reason
    you'd be interested in ballet,
Except that when we jump a fence,
    you've done a grand jété!

Of course one thing that's different
    between your big jump and mine
Is that only if I stretch both knees
    will Miss Bradley say, "It's fine."
She can be very strict, and very stern,
    so it's her I strive to impress,
But today was special because she said
    it's love we must try to express.
Oh, Sugar, I can't wait till morning,
    when I come to clean your stall,
Then I can show you in my toe shoes
    how love can grow so tall!

Chapter 6

The next morning before school I went into the barn with our veterinarian, Dr. Gallagher, who came by early to give Sugar a vaccination and to check his teeth. Dr. Gallagher was actually a lady doctor, and her first name was Rachel. She told me older horses had to get their flu shots every year just like people do. But Sugar really didn't like getting his shots any more than I did. So he didn't look too happy when he saw Dr. Gallagher walk around behind him with a needle. He whinnied all of a sudden and shook his head.

But Dr. Gallagher just rubbed him a little behind his ears and calmed him down. I liked Dr. Gallagher. She was smart, and she told me some really neat stories about horses and about being a horse doctor and all. She said that a long time ago she lived someplace in New York and took care of all of the horses at a big racetrack. She used to check the horses before each race to make sure nobody had given them drugs. After she had finished giving Sugar his shot, Dr. Gallagher told me a sad story about this one horse named Pal Joey, who had raced at that same track before Dr. Gallagher worked there.

"Now, Rosie," she said, closing the door to Sugar's stall, "this was back in the days before we had to test the horses for drugs. What happened to Pal Joey couldn't happen today. He was a beautiful animal, and he had one long white streak on his nose like Sugar does. His owner was a very cruel man named Buster Shaw. Buster was a no-good rascal. He overtrained and pushed that horse something terrible. Now, a racehorse can't help but hurt himself in training sometimes. Training a horse to race is just not a natural thing to do. When Pal Joey strained one of his knees, Buster gave him a very dangerous kind of painkiller to try to get him to the Kentucky Derby. And until the last race of the season up in Saratoga, Pal Joey certainly did look like a sure winner. But those drugs didn't really help his knee, and in that last race Pal Joey went lame when he was out in front, coming down the stretch. So he never made it to the finish line."

I cried, "He went lame?"

Dr. Gallagher put her arm around my shoulder, and then she said, "That's right. The poor thing was in the lead through the whole race, but then his legs just went out from under him."

I asked Dr. Gallagher, "What happened to his creepy owner? Did he go to jail?"

As we walked out of the barn together, Dr. Gallagher said, "Well, no one was ever able to prove that Buster Shaw had done it. But not long after that we started testing the horses before each race, so it could never happen again. You see, Rosie, racehorses have to train just like athletes, so Pal Joey made it safer for all the other horses that came after him."

"So your job was to protect the racehorses?" I asked.

Dr. Gallagher smiled and said, "That's right, Rosie."

I told her, "That sounds like a really terrific job."

I walked Dr. Gallagher to her car, and then waved good-bye when she drove off. My mom ran out of the house like she was in a big hurry or something. She was already on her way to work this morning. I told you she drives one of the school buses for Riverview High School. My mom had to leave an hour before my bus would even come down our road. As she was getting in the car, she yelled to me, "I'm late, Rosie. You have a good day in school. I'll see you when you get home."

My dad walked me to the bus stop. He does that every year on the first day of school. I always hate the first day, and he always makes a joke about the two of us just taking a walk to the bus stop to see what color the bus is. But it's always the same bus, and, of course, it's always yellow. You'd think that my dad would know by now, but every year he makes the same joke all over again. I go to Riverview Elementary School, and we never find out who's in our class and who our new teacher will be until we get there. Everybody goes to the auditorium first thing, and then the teachers call our names.

All during the bus ride to school and all the while I was sitting in the auditorium waiting for my name to be called, I kept thinking about Pal Joey and how glad I was that horses nowadays were safe from people like that Buster Shaw. I wondered what it was inside people that made some of them cruel like that. That drove me crazy, because I never heard of a cruel horse. Deidre Larson's horse, Big Shot, can be pretty mean, but that's only because Big Shot is almost always in a bad mood. I'd probably be in a bad mood, too, if I had to live with Deidre and her twin sister, Karen. They would really drive me crazy. They're both friends of Cynthia's, and they don't know anything about taking care of horses. One time they let Big Shot eat a whole bag of oats, and his stomach almost exploded.

Deidre, Karen, and Cynthia were sitting two rows in front of me in the auditorium. Cynthia had her hair in a bun, and she was giggling in between Deidre and Karen. She turned around and sort of whispered really loud, "I heard Miss Bradley's not gonna let you take ballet any-more, Rosie. She says you're starting to look like your horse."

"Yeah, Rosie," said Deidre, "You've got bowed legs like Sugar."

Karen said, "Her face looks like Sugar's too."

I knew that they had to be lying, and so I made be-lieve I didn't hear what they were saying. Then I heard my name called over the loudspeaker. I was going to be in Mr. Howell's fifth-grade class. I'd never had a man for a teacher before, and so I wasn't too sure whether I was going to like Mr. Howell or not. When I saw him standing at the front of the auditorium, I thought he sort of looked like an owl, with big bushy eyebrows and eyes that almost seemed like they were going to pop out of his head. But Mr. Howell turned out to be nice. Except he took my picture when I first walked into his classroom.

Mr. Howell took everybody's picture. He was a pho-tographer, and he said he was going to put our pictures up on the bulletin board for Parent's Night. I always hate having my picture taken, and so I wasn't too happy about that camera. Once we were all in the classroom and sitting at our desks, Mr. Howell put his camera on his desk and stood in front of the blackboard. Then he told us, "I'll be taking more shots of you later on, so we can show your parents what wonderful angels all of you are when you're here in school."

Everybody groaned when he said that. When I looked around the room, I knew most of the kids in class. Emily was sitting two rows behind me. She looked sort of sad. But that was just because Emily tried not to smile so people wouldn't see her braces. I knew she was happy that we were in the same class this year. I was sure glad Cynthia Anderson wasn't in my class like she was last year. But just when I was thinking that, the door opened, and the principal of the school, Mrs. Harrison, brought Cynthia into the classroom. Cynthia was getting switched to Mr. Howell's class because someone sent her to the wrong room by mistake.

Mr. Howell grabbed his camera and took Cynthia's picture with a flashbulb. Then he told her to sit at the desk that was right next to mine. When she saw me, Cynthia batted her eyes and gave me this big phony smile. Unless Mr. Howell let us change our seats later, I was going to be stuck sitting next to Cynthia for this whole year!

While Mr. Howell was passing out books on the other side of the classroom, Cynthia leaned over toward me and whispered, "What I was trying to tell you before, Rosie, is that you're in big trouble because Miss Bradley says you have bowed legs from riding, and she's not going to let you take her class tomorrow."

"How do you know, Cynthia?" I asked.

"Because Miss Bradley called my mom to complain about me riding Tarzan. And she wanted to know who else in our ballet class rode horses. Some people can get bowed legs from their horses. Didn't you know that?"

I asked Cynthia, "What about you? Is Miss Bradley going to let you take class?"

"Oh, sure," she said. "My mom worked everything out with her. I get to take class and ride."

Now I couldn't tell if Cynthia was lying or not. But I knew I didn't have bowed legs. I was pretty sure, anyway. I mean, if I wanted to , I could make my knees touch. In the afternoon, though, during recess, we all went outside to the playground, and I asked Emily if she thought my legs were bowed. But Emily said she couldn't tell because I had my pants on over my legs. "Well, I'm certainly not gonna take my pants off out here," I told her.

Stephen Archer and some of his friends were standing close to us at the side of the playground by the monkey bars, and he'd heard me say that. I knew from Stephen's face that he wasn't going to let me get away with it. He said with this loud voice, "Oh, go ahead, Rosie. You can take them off. We'd all love to see you take your pants off."

He started laughing like he thought what he'd said was just the funniest thing in the world or something. I was embarrassed and all, but I told him, "You know, Stephen, you might think that you're hot stuff. I mean, you play all the sports in school, and you even dance. But you've really got rocks inside of your head instead of brains."

Stephen sure did prove that later, on the way home in the school bus. He and his best friend, Jeremy Hitchcock, were in the backseat, and they set off a firecracker right there inside the bus. The noise was so loud, it hurt my ears, and it was really smelly, like a stink bomb. The bus driver pulled over to the side of the road and stopped the bus. Then he turned around and asked us who had done it. But before anyone said anything, Stephen and Jeremy decided to give themselves up. They came to the front of the bus and confessed to the driver. Now they have to go to the principal's office tomorrow, and they might even get thrown out of school. Anyway, because of them and that dumb firecracker, I was late getting home from school.

My mom wasn't home, and my dad was down at the vegetable stand. That's where I worked after school when I didn't have a ballet class. I usually took class three or four days a week, but today was a Tuesday, and I didn't have class on Tuesdays. I started to go into my room to change into my old clothes, but before I did, I decided to check my knees in the mirror in my parents' bedroom. There's this really long mirror on the back of the door to my mother's closet. So I stood in front of it and pulled down the pants that I'd worn to school.

"Oh, no!" I said out loud to myself. "They *are* bowed. I've got bowed legs!"

When I squeezed my knees together, or bent them in a plié, they didn't look so bad. I decided that I'd ask my mom to look at them after dinner, and so I changed and spent the rest of the afternoon with my dad out at the stand. He was in a pretty jolly mood, and he was whistling the whole time because the weather was still warm, and he didn't have to put smoke pots in the fields or anything.

Plus my mom was making a pot roast for dinner, and that's my dad's favorite meal. Sherlock followed us from the stand up to the house, and when he ran ahead of us to the front door, my dad said, "Sherlock smells roast. Nothing else could make him run like that." Sherlock turned around at the front door and barked at us to hurry up, and I just barked right back at him.

After we finally sat down at the dinner table, my dad kept feeding Sherlock pieces of pot roast right from his plate, and I told my mom all about school and my new teacher, and about how Stephen and Jeremy had set off that firecracker on the bus. My mom always waits until we're having dessert to talk about anything really serious. So after she brought out cherry pie from the kitchen, she asked me straight out, "Rosalie, do you still want to become a ballerina when you grow up? Are you enjoying Miss Bradley's class as much as you did last year?"

Just by the way she'd asked me those two questions right in a row, I knew she meant business. I mean, she wasn't joking around with me or anything, and all of a sudden my dad stopped horsing around with Sherlock and sort of looked at me like he was waiting to hear what I was going to say. What I said was "Well, I'm going to be a veterinarian. And I'm going to be a ballerina too."

My mom said, "A veterinarian?"

My dad raised his eyebrows and said, "What's this I hear? I thought you were going to be my jockey for the Kentucky Derby?"

"Oh, Dad," I said. "You're joking, right?"

My dad knew I was never going to be a jockey. He was only trying to get my goat. That's what he called it when he teased me like that, and I'd always tell him that I didn't have a goat for him to get. I said, "I'd much rather be a doctor and take care of horses, like Dr. Gallagher."

My mom said to me, "Sometimes, Rosalie, we can't always do all of the things we might want to in this world. Are you sure you haven't changed your mind about dancing?"

"Oh, honestly, Mom," I said, "why are you asking me all of these questions? Am I supposed to decide my whole life tonight or something?"

Then she said, "Miss Bradley called me today . . ."

My mom looked like she was trying to think of what

to say next, but I blurted out, "Oh, no! Cynthia was right. What did Miss Bradley say? Do I have bowed legs?"

"Oh, good heavens! She didn't say anything about your legs, Rosalie. Miss Bradley thinks you're very talented, but she's worried that if you continue riding Sugar as much as you do, your muscles may not develop properly for dancing. You use different muscles in your back and legs whenever you ride. And they're the wrong muscles for dancing. So Miss Bradley wondered if you might not cut down on all the riding for a while, and see how you feel about it."

I said, "I already know how I feel about it. I feel lousy. That's how I feel. Cynthia said that she's allowed to ride and dance too. How come she's not using the wrong muscles when she goes riding Tarzan all over the place?"

My mom said, "Well, if that's so, Miss Bradley may not think Cynthia is as talented as you are. It doesn't sound like Cynthia really wants to be a ballerina. She doesn't seem to love dancing as much as you do."

"But I love riding too," I told her. I also knew how Sugar would feel if I were to stop riding him. He'd go nuts if I didn't ride him. But my mom seemed to be telling me that was just what I was supposed to do. I said, "That's not fair!"

"Well, you think about it, Rosalie," she said. "With winter coming and the cold weather, you won't be wanting to ride as much anyway. And if you try to do both, ride and dance, you might hurt yourself. That's what I worry about."

My dad said, "Sometimes we have to do things we really don't much want to do, Rosalie."

"Oh, fiddlesticks!" I cried. "How can this be happening to me?" I didn't even finish my dessert. I just ran upstairs to my room and shut the door behind me.

What else could I do?

Chapter 7

"I didn't sleep too hot last night," I told my mom the next morning at breakfast. "And neither did Sugar. He had a nightmare. I heard him scream like he does when he has one of his bad dreams."

My mom was standing over the stove, making pancakes, and my dad was sitting at the kitchen table with me. He said, "Oh, you must have been dreaming, Rosie. I didn't hear him." My mom came over and put a big plate of pancakes on the table. My dad already had his fork in his hand, and he was ready to stab one of those pancakes, but first he looked up and asked my mom, "Did you hear Sugar last night?"

My mom said, "I didn't hear anything last night, except your snoring. If Sugar was making noise like Rosie says, maybe he was trying to tell you to quiet down."

My dad didn't say anything. He doesn't like to admit he snores. So he just laughed and asked me to pass him the maple syrup.

Then my mom sat down at the table. Before she'd even looked at her plate, she asked me, "Rosalie, have you given some thought to what we talked about last night? Do you think you might want to hold off on the riding for a while?"

I could tell that's what my mom wanted me to do, even though she didn't actually come out and say so. She didn't have to. My mom was always worrying about me. After she heard from Uncle Max about me falling off Sugar when we rode into town the other day, I knew she probably thought that dancing was safer for me than riding.

I said, "Oh, Mom, I don't know. How am I supposed to know what to do? But I'll bet that's why Sugar had that nightmare last night. He's worried that I might not be able to ride him again for a while."

All of a sudden my stomach sort of told me that I really didn't want any more pancakes. My dad said, "Don't be silly, Rosalie. How would Sugar know? Last time I looked, he was still a horse. Eat your pancakes before they get cold."

"I'm not hungry," I told him.

I sounded pretty grumpy even to me, and it got really quiet at the table for a while. I picked up my fork and sort of mashed my pancakes in the syrup on my plate. Sometimes when my parents get upset with me and don't say anything, it's even worse than if they would just yell at me. Finally my mom said, "I think I may have an idea you'll like, Rosalie. If you give Sugar a rest this week, I'll see about getting tickets for us to go to see a ballet at the theater up in Brighton Falls this weekend. I know they're doing a production of *Sleeping Beauty* at the college there. How does that sound to you?"

"Great!" I told her. I'd never seen a ballet before except on television. So I was really excited at first about going with my mom. But then I remembered the part about not riding for the rest of the week, and I said, "I don't think Sugar's going to think it's so great, though, Mom."

She just said, "Well, you think about it, dear."

I kept thinking about it all day in school, and even after, when I went to my ballet class. I couldn't make up my mind what to do. I mean, it was wasn't like I wouldn't see Sugar every day and take care of him and all. But it seemed like all of a sudden I was supposed to choose between riding and taking ballet, and it didn't seem fair to me. I was afraid that Miss Bradley was going to say something to me before class. Today she'd opened up the curtains so we could see ourselves in the mirror again. The sun was really bright outside, and light was streaming in through the windows onto the wood floor. We wouldn't be wearing our toe shoes this afternoon. This was our regular class, and so there were a few boys in the studio too.

Before starting the barre exercises, Miss Bradley stood in front and spoke to the whole class. While she was talking, she looked at each of us, one by one, right in the eye. Miss Bradley didn't exactly say anything about horses or riding. But she did say if we girls wanted to be ballerinas, we'd have to work harder and make some pretty big sacrifices. Then Miss Bradley looked at Stephen Archer and said, "Now, that goes for you boys too. Those of you who really want to become dancers will have to give more and more of your time. That may mean you'll have less time for some of your other activities, like sports. Sooner or later you may find you have some very difficult decisions to make. Ballet is a terribly demanding art. When you're older, you may decide that it's not for you. There is nothing to be ashamed of if that's what you decide. Ballet is not for everyone."

I liked Miss Bradley a lot, but I didn't like the way she looked at me when she said that stuff about difficult decisions. At least Cynthia Anderson wasn't taking class today. She hadn't been in school either. Someone said she stayed home sick. I was just glad I didn't have to see her today. After Miss Bradley was done talking to us, I ran to the corner of the studio and scuffed my ballet slippers in the rosin box. Then I found a spot at one of the portable barres in the middle of the room. I don't know why, but my body wouldn't do anything I wanted it to. I looked in the mirror and it seemed like I was turning into a total spastic. I was lucky I had the barre to hold on to or I would have fallen flat on my face.

Just before the end of the barre exercises, Miss Bradley walked up behind me and said, "You're not concentrating today, Rosie." Then she sort of yelled at everybody, "Stop looking in that mirror. For the rest of this class, just for today, I want all of you to keep looking toward those windows at the end of the studio. The sun is going to be your focus. Okay? I want you to make believe that somewhere out there someone you really, really love is walking toward you in the sunshine, and you just can't wait to see him. Or her. Now, let's move the barres out of the way and go on to the center work."

The sunshine made it hot in the studio, and by the time we got to the big jumps, I was sweating like crazy. I kept looking out the window and wondering whether or not Sugar would still love me if I stopped riding him. Miss Bradley told us to cross the floor two at a time for glissade grande jetés—they were really big jumps, where you sort of made a scissors in the air with your legs, stretching them as far as they would go. Plus you had to keep switching legs, first jumping off the left leg, and then off the right.

I got a big surprise when I saw Stephen Archer get on

line beside me for this step. Why in the world was Stephen standing next to me? We were in front of the line at the corner of the studio, and Stephen made me even more nervous than I already was. It wasn't like we were partners or we'd be holding hands or anything. Each of us had to do the jumps on our own. But just knowing he was right next to me made me feel kind of weird inside, and so I tried to make believe he wasn't there. Miss Bradley asked the pianist to play a grande allegro. That was a pretty fast tempo. After the first time Stephen and I went across the studio, Miss Bradley yelled at us, "Don't look so gloomy, you two. *Allegro* means full of cheer. These are supposed to be happy steps. Don't think about jumping up. Just push away from the floor. The floor is your best friend."

Then Miss Bradley made us do pushups. She said, "The way your arms feel when you're pushing up is the same way your legs should feel when you jump."

The way my arms felt, I sure didn't think that floor was my friend or anything. Stephen and I tried doing the steps again, but we didn't look too happy. Miss Bradley told us to try skipping across the floor to the windows. That turned out to be fun because I really loved to skip—and I almost beat Stephen! Then Miss Bradley said, "Now try the jumps again, but think of them like you're skipping."

This time our jumps were better, and Miss Bradley told us so. When we were standing and waiting at the side of the studio, Stephen whispered to me, "I didn't know you could jump that high, Rosie. You almost jump higher than I do. If you were taller, you'd be a good basketball player."

I knew that Stephen was just trying to be nice, but I still get pretty touchy sometimes about being such a shrimp. So all I said was "I don't like basketball."

He sort of wrinkled up his nose and made a funny face at me. But Miss Bradley saw him. She said, "That's very good, Stephen. Why don't you do that again, so the rest of the class can see what you're doing."

Stephen can be a real clown when he wants to, but I don't think he liked hearing everybody laugh at him after he wrinkled up his face again. But then Miss Bradley told all of us to make faces. "You see," she said, "when we dance, we have to use the muscles in our faces just like we use the muscles in the rest of our bodies. So we need to exercise our faces and develop those muscles too. Now try wiggling your ears like this. And raise your eyebrows so it feels like you're lifting your whole scalp right off the top of your head."

Miss Bradley had us do some pretty weird stuff sometimes. Once she even made us sing out loud while we were doing some of the steps. She told us that dancers had to learn how to breathe and use their voices just like singers do. At the end of class we clapped for her like we always do. But she told us to quiet down. Then she said, "We're very lucky this year, because the high school is going to let us use the auditorium in December for a production of *The Nutcracker*. I'll be watching all of you very closely in class for the next few weeks while I decide whom to cast in each of the roles. You all worked very well today. Thank you for coming."

I hurried out of the studio past Miss Bradley and went to the dressing room. After I changed my clothes and all, I rode home with Emily and her mom, Mrs. Wright. Emily lives near where Stephen lives on Mountain Valley Road. You might remember I live on that same road. Since Emily and Stephen and I were neighbors, our folks usually took turns dropping us off and picking us up from class. Only Emily didn't have a father anymore because he died in a car accident a few years ago. I felt sorry for Emily because I couldn't even imagine how I'd feel if I ever lost my dad. Mrs. Wright had Emily's four-year-old sister, Ellen, in the front seat with her, and so the three of us older kids had to sit in the back. We were practically sitting on top of each other because our dance stuff and our schoolbooks wouldn't fit in the trunk. I really didn't feel too hot about being so cramped.

After we were on the road, Stephen told Mrs. Wright he was sure he was going to get a role in *The Nutcracker*. I could hardly believe it! All of a sudden he sounded like he thought he was Mikhail Baryshnikov or something. I said to him, "I thought you hated ballet."

But Stephen said dancing made him better at sports. "It's good for your coordination," he told me. "Some of the guys who play football for Riverview High are taking ballet classes from Miss Bradley this year."

I guess that sometimes I can get pretty shy around boys. I mean, I never know what to say that they won't tease me about. So sitting there between Stephen and Emily, I didn't say much for a while. I hardly even laughed when Stephen made his funny face again, but for a second I sort of liked him, even though I still thought he had rocks in his head. He bragged about being called down to the principal's office and how he got off easy. He said the principal just warned him about setting off more firecrackers on the bus, and then called his parents. Emily asked if he was worried about what his mom and dad would say when he got home. But Stephen said, "No. They don't care what I do."

The funny thing, though, was the way Stephen said that his parents didn't care what he did. It sounded like he was sorry, and sort of wished they did care. I couldn't imagine my parents not caring like that. I mean, if I ever got called down to the principal's office, my mom and dad would go crazy. That's for sure. I don't know what they'd

do. There was this one time, when I sort of talked back to my mom in the barn, and my dad hollered at me and said I couldn't ride Sugar for a month. Later, though, after I told my mom how sorry I was and how I'd never talk back again, she got my dad to change his mind about me not riding.

But I never forgot how scared I was, and that was sort of the way I was feeling now with my mom trying to get me not to ride and all. It was like I had done something wrong, only I didn't know what it was. I couldn't wait to get home to see Sugar. When we turned onto Mountain Valley Road, Mrs. Wright looked at me in the mirror and said, "You're awfully quiet today, Rosalie. Are you feeling all right?"

Mrs. Wright was older than my mom, and she had all of this gray hair. She was pretty nice, I guess, but I wasn't going to tell her all of the stuff that I've been telling you about. No way. I just said, "I'm fine," and then I thanked her when she dropped me off in front of my house.

I raced up the stairs to my room and changed my clothes. My mom said that I should start my homework before dinner, but I took my diary from my night table and snuck outside to the barn. Sometimes I sit up in the hayloft when I want to think about things. It's really quiet up there, and I can look down on Sugar's stall. When I saw him, I told him I'd come down to brush him in a minute. But first I had to write something in my diary.

It was another letter I wrote. But this time I just made believe I was talking to Sugar. When I finished, I didn't feel much better, but I went down to his stall and read it out loud to him anyway.

Oh, Sugar, I see you
lowering your head,
after hearing about ballet
and all that's been said.

Please lift your ears
so that I can confide
the trouble I have deciding
whether or not I should ride.

You know that my heart
is all taut and tense,
because having to choose
just doesn't make sense.

Now my teacher is special,
you've heard that before,
but she says I should be
willing to sacrifice more.

When we ride you can feel
　　my legs holding on tight,
　　　　but the muscles that hold you,
　　　　　　I've been told are not right.

Oh, I know how you feel,
　　and I can't change that,
　　　　but believe me, Sugar,
　　　　　　I am not an old rat!

After I was through reading, Sugar stamped the floor of the stall and shook his head at me. He was saying, "Oh, hurry up and brush me, Rosie."

Then I heard my mom calling me for dinner. I promised Sugar I'd come back as fast as I could. Before I left, I could see that he wasn't too happy with me, and I didn't blame him one bit, because I wasn't too happy with me either.

Chapter 8

After I left Sugar in the barn and went inside the house, I decided that I had to do what my mom wanted and not ride for the rest of the week, even though it made me sad. My mom bought us tickets to see the ballet in Brighton Falls on Saturday night, and she said I could ask Emily to come with us, because my dad said he didn't want to go. But by the time Saturday morning came, I didn't much want to go either. Sugar was getting sadder and sadder about us not being able to go out together to ride our favorite trails. When I ran out the back door to brush him in the morning, I was trying to think of something I could do to cheer him up. Then, just when I was starting down the porch steps, I almost stepped on Ali, our cat.

I forgot to tell you about him. Ali is my mom's tom-cat. Ali's orange and looks sort of like a big pumpkin with fur. My mom found him one morning. He'd been beaten up by some mean old raccoon. Ali still has some scars on his face, and he's got only one ear now. Since he's always getting into fights, we named him after my dad's all-time favorite boxer, Muhammad Ali. Ali's never allowed in the house because my dad's allergic to cats. So Ali stays in the barn on most nights. Only sometimes he goes off for weeks to hunt and to look for girl cats. My dad says Ali may not be much of a house cat, but he's the world champion mouse cat, because he loves to catch the field mice that live on our farm. Whenever he catches a mouse, Ali brings it up to the house and leaves it for us on the porch steps. And that's just what he was doing when I almost tripped over him.

Ali was lying on the steps with this little mouse between his paws, and I practically had to do a grande jeté just to get around him. I sort of jumped off from the top of the steps, and I was sure I was going to fall. But just as I screamed and went flying in the air, Uncle Max came by surprise and was right there at the bottom of the steps in time to catch me. I couldn't believe it. I hadn't seen Uncle Max when I first came out the door. It was like all of a sudden he was my partner in ballet class and I was just leaping into his arms. He swung me around by the waist and said, "Careful there, Rosie. You better save some of that energy of yours for Sugar. Wait just a minute. You don't look like you're ready to ride. Where are your riding boots?"

Sometimes I do things, and I don't know why I do them. Honest. I really don't know. So when Uncle Max asked me why I wasn't ready to go riding yet this morning, my arms just sort of flew up around his neck, all by themselves, and held on to him. I mean I wasn't crying or anything. Only I couldn't seem to make any words come up out of my throat. It was Saturday morning, and Uncle Max had come to give me and Sugar another cavalletti lesson. While I was holding on to my uncle's neck, Sherlock came over to us and started barking at Ali and that mouse. What a racket! All of that crazy barking in my ears made it hard to think, and my head felt more confused than ever.

When Uncle Max put me down, I told him, "I can't ride today. I'm sorry, Uncle Max."

"What's this?" he asked. "What do you mean, you can't ride?"

"Well," I said, "it's just that I promised Mom I wouldn't ride this week."

I looked down and felt worse than that poor old mouse Ali left on the step. And I was afraid Uncle Max was going to be mad because he'd made the trip all the way out here this morning for nothing. My mom forgot to tell him I wasn't going to have my lesson. But Uncle Max just took his corncob pipe out of his mouth and said, "Don't worry about that, Rosie. We can ride another day. Where's your mom this morning? I want some of her black coffee." After I told him that she was still in the kitchen, Uncle Max gave me a pat on the back and walked past me up the steps and into the house.

I turned around and started walking out toward the barn. Then I saw my dad in the driveway, unloading some big boxes and lumber from our pickup truck. He stopped what he was doing when he saw me and pointed up to the sky. "Look, over there. Can you see them, Rosie?" I had to put my hand over my eyes to block the sun. Then I saw this long stream of little black specks high above the trees. Those specks were geese, and pretty soon my dad and I heard them honking over our heads. There were thousands of them! They were from Canada, and they were flying south for the winter. You might not know about geese, but they migrate every year at about this time when the leaves start changing colors. My dad and I just stood there for a while, and we sort of said good-bye to them as they passed us and disappeared behind the trees on the other side of our house.

The funny thing was that while we were watching the geese, I almost forgot how crummy I felt. It was just peaceful seeing them way up there in the sky, and I didn't have to think about much of anything else. Plus my dad had his arm around my shoulders, and that made me feel good. But then, after the geese were gone, my dad told me, "Rosie, I want you to stay out of the barn today. I've got an awful lot of work to finish out there, and I can't have you in the way."

"What about Sugar?" I asked. "I have to clean his stall and brush him, and then—"

My dad didn't give me a chance to say anything else. He put his hand on the top of my head and said, "You can go take care of Sugar right now, and then put him down in the lower field for the afternoon."

I went into the barn and gave Sugar a carrot, and he gobbled it right out of my hand. Then Sugar did this thing he does sometimes, where he sort of curled his lips up in front of his teeth. It was his way of smiling. I whispered to him, "We've got to think of something, or both of us are going to go crazy!"

Sugar spent the whole afternoon in the field, and I worked at the vegetable stand out on the road until my mom called me to the house. I had to take another bath and get ready to go to the ballet. My mom made me get dressed up. She told me to wear my yellow dress that I only ever wore to church. My mom sure seemed a lot more excited about going tonight than I was. The two of us ate dinner at the kitchen table before my dad came in from work, and my mom kept telling me what a wonderful time we were going to have and all. But I wasn't so sure anymore.

Before we left for the ballet, I went out to say goodbye to Sugar, but my dad still wouldn't let me go into the barn. He stopped me at the door and said, "You can't go in there yet, Rosie. I'm not finished working. You can say good night to Sugar after you and your mom get back from the ballet."

"But, Dad," I said.

"Just hurry along now," he told me. "Your mom's ready to leave."

My mom wasn't actually ready to leave. She always takes forever to get ready. By the time we left the house and picked up Emily and drove all the way to Brighton Falls, we were almost late for the ballet. The theater was inside an old brick building that you could hardly see because the walls were all covered over with ivy. It was on the campus of the state college, and it took us an hour to find the theater, because my mom got lost. There was this billboard out front and a picture of these two dancers who looked just like a prince and princess. He was lifting her way up over his head, and underneath them there were these big letters that went like this:

ONE WEEK ONLY
THE SLEEPING BEAUTY
WITH SPECIAL GUESTS
FROM RUSSIA'S KIROV BALLET
NATALIA CHERNOVA AND MIKHAIL VASILIKOV

After we parked our car and went inside, an usher with a flashlight had to take us to our seats because the lights were out and the music was already starting. A big red curtain went up just as we sat down. I sat between my mom and Emily, and I could see the whole stage because nobody was sitting in the row ahead of us. There were all of these lights with different colors shining down onto the stage, and the dancers were wearing these really beautiful costumes. It was like they were inside this magic kingdom, and we were right there with them the whole time.

I already knew the story of *Sleeping Beauty*, but the way they danced it made it seem really special. You probably know the story too. It's the one about the beautiful princess who pricks her finger and goes to sleep for a hundred years. There's this wicked old fairy who tries to kill the princess with an evil spell. But then a good fairy comes along and puts another spell on her, so the princess doesn't die. She goes to sleep instead. After a hundred years this handsome prince wakes her up with a kiss, and they get married, of course, and live happily ever after.

The part that I liked best came near the beginning, when the princess was having her birthday party, before she pricked her finger and went to sleep. There were these four princes who came to her party, and the princess took a rose from each prince and then twirled around like she was really excited. Later, she had to stay up on one leg and balance that way while the princes took turns holding her hand. My mom told me this part of the ballet was called the "Rose Adagio." I'd heard the music before because there were a couple of times when Miss Bradley asked the pianist to play the same music in class. Only now the violins in the orchestra were playing it, instead of the piano. The ballerina looked like she was sparkling there in a silvery pool of light. She was wearing a shiny pink tutu, and she had a crown on her head. While I watched her balance on the tip of her toe shoe, I wondered if I'd ever learn how to keep my balance as long as she did. She had her arms up in a circle over her head as each prince approached to offer her his hand. She was sort of smiling, but when the last of those princes held out his hand to her, she looked pretty shaky. Her legs and arms were sort of trembling from the strain and all.

Emily said right out loud, "She's gonna fall over!"

But the ballerina didn't fall, and I told Emily to keep her voice down. She kept talking during the performance. The ballerina was one of the Russian dancers whose picture we saw in front of the theater. She just threw her arms up over her head and kept dancing. The whole audience clapped for her, and I heard this man behind me yell, "Brava! Brava!" Then, a little while later, the evil fairy came along to the birthday party with a black hood covering her head so nobody knew who she was. She gave the princess a big spindle of thread, and that was how the princess pricked her finger. Then she fell down and went to sleep, and everybody else in the kingdom fell asleep too. Boy, that ballerina was graceful even when she fell down, and everyone cheered and clapped for her again.

She was so beautiful. I mean, not just the way she looked, but the way she moved her whole body. During the intermission my mom and Emily and I went out to the lobby and stood around for a little while. I told Emily, "Someday I'm going to dance like that ballerina. I just know I am." I felt awfully dumb after I said that. But Emily just said that she didn't see how anybody could ever get to be that good. I said, "They do the same steps that we do in class. But they know how to dance them a lot better than we do. Those Russian dancers may be more graceful than we are, but that's only because they've been studying longer than we have."

A bell started ringing to tell everybody the intermission was over, and that was when I saw Stephen Archer and his parents coming toward us from across the lobby.

His mom and dad stopped to say hello to my mom, and Stephen looked like he didn't want us to see him at first. He was wearing a coat and tie and all, and I thought to myself that his parents must have made him come to the ballet tonight. But when my mom asked Stephen if he was enjoying himself, he said that he was having a really great time, and that he thought that Russian ballerina was terrific. He sounded like he meant it, and when we went back to our seats, I asked Emily, "Do you think Stephen really likes ballet now?"

Emily said, "I think he really likes Cynthia. He's always looking at her in class, and I saw her over at his house yesterday. They were playing basketball in his driveway."

"No way!" I said. But Emily swore she'd seen them together. As the lights started going down, I felt pretty weird, and I just wondered to myself how Emily could have known Stephen was looking at Cynthia all the time unless Emily was looking at him too. All I could say to Emily was "I still think Stephen's dumb, and if he wants to play basketball with Cynthia Anderson, that just proves how dumb he really is."

Emily said, "Oh, you're just jealous." Then my mom leaned over and told us to quiet down because the orchestra had started playing. The end of the ballet turned out to be even better than the beginning, because the ending was so happy. I always like happy endings better than sad ones.

The prince and princess got married and everyone in the kingdom went to their wedding and danced. When the curtain came down, we all clapped like mad, and then the curtain went right back up again. The ballerina who was the princess was given a big bouquet of red roses. When she came to the front of the stage to bow, you could tell that she was wearing tons of makeup. I mean, she had these really gigantic false eyelashes. I still thought that she was beautiful, but she looked all tired out when you saw her close up.

By the time my mom drove us home and dropped Emily off at her house, it was almost midnight, and I was tired too. But my dad had said that I could say good night to Sugar, and so as soon as my mom and I got out of the car, I ran straight to the barn to find him. But when I first went inside, I got this really giant surprise. My dad had made a ballet studio right there inside the barn! He'd cleared a big space on the floor and put up mirrors and everything. My dad was hammering a barre to the wall, so he didn't hear me come in at first.

When he turned around, he put down his hammer and smiled at me. He looked really proud, like he does after he fixes something himself. He said, "Your mom and I thought you might want to be in here with Sugar when you practice your dancing, Rosie. What do you think?"

I just whooped for joy and ran over and jumped all the

way into my dad's arms. I cried, "Oh, Dad, you're terrific. I can't believe it!"

But then I saw Sugar. He had his head hanging down over the door of his stall, and his eyes looked so sad when they saw me. I said, "What's wrong, Sugar? Don't you like it?" He shook his head, and I tried to explain to him, "Look. At least we can spend more time together now, even if I still can't go riding for a while."

My dad said, "I don't think Sugar was too pleased about all the hammering out here tonight."

Sugar put his ears back and looked at himself in one of the mirrors in front of his stall. Then he just shook his head at me again and whinnied, as if he couldn't believe what had happened to his barn. He sure didn't look like he wanted to hear about what a good time I'd had at the ballet, and I wasn't about to tell him either. I just wanted to go to sleep, and when I finally put my head down on my pillow that night, I was hoping I wouldn't wake up for a hundred years.

walks in the fields. He even tried to make believe he was happy for me sometimes, like when I snuck out to the barn and put on my toe shoes without him knowing, and then surprised him by going up on my toes and looking over the door of his stall. But he just wasn't himself anymore, and neither was I. It was like I was split in two! Even though I might not have been as good at riding as I was at ballet, I still loved to ride almost as much as I loved to dance. But I loved Sugar way more than riding or dancing.

Everything was getting so mixed up inside my head that it was really hard just to figure all of this stuff out, especially since I loved my mom and my dad too. I didn't want to disappoint either of them, because they both worked really hard and made lots of sacrifices for me. I guess I was being kind of selfish, and I felt guilty too, but it was just impossible to choose between Sugar and my parents and the things that I loved doing most. But then, just before Thanksgiving, everything got even worse, and I knew I was going to have to choose, once and for all.

There was one really cold and nasty Saturday afternoon, and it was raining cats and dogs, and horses too. The farrier had come to put some winter shoes on Sugar. Our farrier's name was Mr. Withers, and I used to think his name was sort of funny because *withers* is the name of that part of a horse's back that's right up there between his shoulder blades. Mr. Withers told me one time that there

Chapter 9

$\mathcal{I}$ didn't know what to do. I really didn't. I knew that my dad had gone to an awful lot of trouble to build that studio in the barn for me. So it wasn't as if I could tell him I didn't want it and I wasn't going to dance anymore. If I'd said that to my dad, his feelings would have been hurt. So I didn't say anything to anybody, and for the next few weeks I didn't ride Sugar. Not even once. My mom rode him a few times, and so did my dad. But it was like I was the only one who could see how sad Sugar was about us not riding together.

Whenever I practiced my dancing in the barn, Sugar watched me from his stall, and there was always this sadness in his eyes even though he didn't cry tears or anything. But I knew that he was crying on the inside. Sugar still liked it when I brushed him and when I led him for was a mule in every horse, and he said he was just as stubborn as an old mule too. Mr. Withers was about the oldest person I knew. I mean, he must have been almost a hundred years old. My mom said she thought Mr. Withers might be a little bit touched in the head. That was because he mumbled a lot when he worked, and you couldn't tell whether he was talking to himself or the horse. But my dad said Mr. Withers just got himself kicked in the head one too many times by the horses he put shoes on.

I asked Mr. Withers how many times he'd been kicked, and he told me hardly ever. I believed him too, because he was so gentle, and he had a way with horses. They usually did whatever he asked them to do. But when we went out to the barn that afternoon, Sugar had decided that he wasn't going to do anything Mr. Withers asked him to. He started screaming and making this terrible fuss as soon as he saw us, and he wouldn't even come out of his stall.

Mr. Withers backed away from Sugar and asked me, "What in tarnation has got into him, Rosie?"

I told him, "Well, Sugar is upset because we haven't been riding lately. So he thinks that he doesn't need any new shoes this winter."

Mr. Withers pointed to Sugar's pail and said, "He thinks he doesn't need any food either. Look there. He hasn't touched his oats." It was true. Sugar's pail was almost full. Mr. Withers said, "He's trying to tell ya something, and you'd better listen to him, doncha know."

Sugar reared up and kicked the wall of his stall with his hooves. He didn't have his halter on today, and so there was no way for us to get hold of him. I reached down into the pocket of my jeans and found one of Sugar's favorite candies. You probably remember me telling you before how much Sugar likes those red and white Starlight Mints. I crinkled up the cellophane wrapper in my hand, and then Sugar started to calm down. He stuck his head over the door of the stall and took the mint from my hand. After that he was quiet enough for Mr. Withers to put on his halter. Then Mr. Withers led him out of his stall.

Before he put on Sugar's new shoes, Mr. Withers told me, "Like I said, you'd better listen to him. When a horse gets a sadness in him and goes off his food, he can make himself awful sick. Why, a horse can die of a broken heart. I've seen 'em do it. They get a sadness inside, and they won't let go of it, and they won't eat nothin' either. They're awful stubborn animals, doncha know. So you'd best be careful with him."

I promised Mr. Withers I would be careful, and after he'd finished putting new shoes on Sugar, I said good-bye and ran into the house to find my mom. She was in the kitchen, and I told her everything that Mr. Withers had said. She said, "Oh, Rosie. He was just exaggerating. You know how he is. There's no reason for us to be worried about Sugar."

"But, Mom," I told her, "you don't know how sad Sugar is. He didn't eat his oats this morning."

"Well, we'll keep an eye on him, and if we need to, we'll call Dr. Gallagher to have a look at him." I could tell from her expression that I shouldn't say anything else. So I turned around to leave. But my mom said, "Wait a minute, Rosie. Miss Bradley called me a little while ago, and I have some good news for you. She said to tell you that she's giving you a role in *The Nutcracker*. Isn't that great?"

My mom was pretty excited, and my voice got sort of shaky and all when I tried to answer her. "No," I cried. "It's not great. Because I'm quitting ballet! I'm never taking another class."

My mom looked really surprised. She said, "What on earth do you mean, Rosalie?"

My eyes were full of tears, and I ran out of the kitchen as fast as I could. I just yelled back to my mom, "I quit. I quit ballet forever! That's what I mean."

I ran right upstairs to my room and tore down the poster of Baryshnikov from my ceiling. I took down all my other ballet posters too. Then I packed my toe shoes into a box, and later I told my mom I was going to give them away. She didn't try to stop me or anything. She sat on my bed and said, "Rosie, that's fine if that's what you've decided you really want to do. Cynthia Anderson takes your size. You can give your shoes to her. But before you do that, you had better give Miss Bradley a call, and tell her what you've decided. You can call her after dinner."

When I'm really upset, I can't remember everything so well, and so I don't remember what I said to my mom before she left me in my room. But I'm sure I must have said something. A little while later I put on my yellow raincoat and went back outside to the barn. I walked over to Sugar's stall, and I told him, "It's too rainy for us to ride today. But we'll go riding again soon, Sugar. I promise you that. Only first you have to eat."

I scooped up some oats in the palm of my hand and held them out under his nose. Sugar sniffed my fingers and then licked my hand until there were no oats left, and then he went over to his pail and started eating. I whispered to him, "Oh, that's great, Sugar. Now, don't go telling Mom or Dad where I am, okay?"

I climbed up to the hayloft. I already told you that's where I go to think, and I guess I was hiding too. I covered myself up with hay and lay there for a long time. I don't know what time it was. But I could see out through the window, and it was already getting pretty dark. Then I heard my mom ringing the bell for dinner. She has this old cowbell on the porch, and she rings it to tell me and my dad when it's time for dinner. You can hear it all the way from our vegetable stand down the road. I knew I'd have to go in sooner or later, but I wasn't in any hurry because I sure wasn't looking forward to calling Miss Bradley. I didn't know what I was going to say to her.

After a little while I got up and brushed the hay off my clothes. When I started to climb down the ladder, I heard the door open and my mom calling into the barn. "Rosalie, are you in there?" I didn't say anything, but she saw me getting down from the ladder. Then she said, "It's time for dinner. Come on now. Hurry along to the house. Your uncle Max is here, and he wants to talk to you."

It had stopped raining. I followed my mom to the house, and we passed Uncle Max's car in the driveway. I was glad that Uncle Max was here. At least I could tell him that I could have my cavalletti lessons again. My dad and Uncle Max were sitting at the dining room table when my mom and I walked inside. Sherlock and his sister, Shirley, were both underneath the table, waiting for dinner. Their tails were wagging and thumping on the floor. When Uncle Max saw me, he said, "Hi there, Rosie! Come here. I need you to do something for me right away."

I ran over and gave Uncle Max a great big hug. He said, "Hold on a minute. Here you go. I want you to take my car keys and go out to my car for me. There's a box in the trunk. I think you'd better bring it in here before we eat."

I did what Uncle Max said. When I got to the car and opened up the trunk, I found a really big cardboard box. It was heavy, and I had to drag it up the porch steps and then into the house. When Uncle Max saw me with the box, he came over and helped me carry it into the living room.

I asked him, "What's inside, Uncle Max?"

He just said, "Well, Rosie, let's open it up and find out."

My mom and dad had come into the living room, and they were standing there, watching me and Uncle Max. The box was on the floor in front of the couch. I tugged at the top, but it was taped shut. Uncle Max said, "Looks like we're going to need a pair of scissors."

"Here you go," said my mom, and she gave me a pair from the drawer of her desk that was behind the couch. I cut up the tape and tore open the cardboard on top. Inside that box was the weirdest saddle I ever saw in my life. It was all covered up with dust, and it looked like an English saddle that was turned sideways.

I held it up in the air and said, "What is it, Uncle Max?"

Uncle Max said, "It's a saddle, Rosie."

"I know," I said, "but what kind of saddle? I never saw a saddle like this one before."

Uncle Max told me, "Why, it's a sidesaddle. It's the kind of saddle ballerinas rode on for hundreds of years. Fact

is, most women used to ride sidesaddle. I found it up in the attic. It belonged to your aunt Helen before she passed on and I thought you might like to have it. It'll need a spot of cleaning, of course, but the leather's still in mighty fine shape."

"But why does it look so weird, Uncle Max?"

"Come over here, and I'll show you." I put the sidesaddle on the floor and went to where my uncle was sitting on the couch. He opened a book on his lap and showed me a picture of this woman riding sidesaddle. She looked really graceful on her horse, I thought. Uncle Max said, "They rode this way for hundreds of years. You see, both legs come over on the same side of your horse. A smart girl like you, Rosie, ought to be able to get the hang of it in no time."

I turned and asked my mom, "Does this mean that if Sugar and I ride with a sidesaddle, I won't be using the wrong muscles for ballet?"

"That's right," said my mom, "and if you really want to look elegant, I can hem up one of my long woolen riding skirts for you to wear this winter."

"Yippie and yahoo!" I screamed. "I can go riding again, and I can dance too. Thanks, Uncle Max. Thank you so much." Then I just threw both of my arms around his neck and cried, "Oh, wait till I tell Sugar!"

"You can tell him all about it tomorrow, Rosie," said my dad. "It's time for dinner."

Later, after we finished dinner and Uncle Max went home, I went upstairs to my room and did some jumping up and down on my bed. Uncle Max had said before he left that he would come over early in the morning to give me my first lesson on the sidesaddle. I was pretty excited, and I wrote Sugar one more little poem in my diary. When I was done with it, I took my diary with me and went downstairs into the kitchen. I took a carrot out of the refrigerator and snuck out the back door. Then I went in the barn and read Sugar the poem that I had written for him. It went like this:

> Oh, Sugar, wake up. Munch
>   this carrot and listen.
> Something has happened that will
>   make your heart glisten!
>
> Like in *The Sleeping Beauty* I saw
>   the other night,
> Everything somehow has turned out
>   just right.
>
> Now, one nasty old fairy might try
>   to spread doom,

Till along comes the good fairy
   to banish the gloom.

And because she's not kind,
   that bad fairy drops dead,
The prince kisses the princess,
   and forever they're wed.

You're as smart as the dickens,
   and gentle as you are wary,
But can you possibly guess now
   what's made me so merry?

It's a sidesaddle, Sugar,
   so we can roam and ride.
I know you'll quickly get used
   to my legs on one side.

Uncle Max is our fairy goduncle
   for giving us this gift.
He says ballerinas long ago were
   graceful and swift.

There's a light in my heart
   where darkness has been,
Oh, Sugar, now we know
   how both of us will win.

Chapter 10

That's almost all I want to tell you about, except for a few things that happened a little while later. I had a really, really, happy Thanksgiving, and I was really grateful. I mean, I knew I was lucky to have so many people in my family who loved me, like my folks and Uncle Max. He taught me how to ride Sugar sidesaddle, and it was a little bit tricky at first, the way you had to balance with your legs hanging down on one side. It took me and Sugar a while to get used to it too. When Cynthia Anderson saw me riding to ballet class one Saturday afternoon, she tried to make fun of me and my weird saddle. She started calling me the sidesaddle ballerina. She said that it was really dumb to ride sideways and that pretty soon I'd start dancing sideways, too.

But I didn't mind when she said that. At least I was still

riding and dancing. And anyway, Miss Bradley gave me a much better role in *The Nutcracker* than she gave Cynthia. You should have seen her face in class when Miss Bradley announced to everybody which roles we were going to be dancing. When Cynthia heard that I was going to be Clara, she really turned colors. I guess I sort of turned colors too when I heard that Stephen Archer was going to be my prince. That meant I was going to have to hold his hand and everything. But I told myself at least Stephen was about the best dancer of all the boys in my class, and he'd be an okay prince, even if he did have some rocks in his head.

Anyhow, the very last thing I want to tell you happened when the first snowstorm came. It was on a Friday night, so I didn't miss school or anything. But the day after it snowed, Saturday, I had to go to my rehearsal for *The Nutcracker* at Miss Bradley's studio in town, and I wasn't sure my mom would be able to drive me. I mean, there must have been at least two or three feet of snow outside, and there were these really deep drifts. Emily had walked to our house that morning to get a ride to the rehearsal. She was in the ballet too. Miss Bradley asked Emily to be one of the soldiers in *The Nutcracker* because there weren't enough boys to dance all of the roles. Anyway, Emily and I were waiting in the kitchen when my mom came in and said, "Put on your coats, girls. The roads have been plowed so we can go into town. Before we leave, Rosalie, your father has something he wants to show you out in the barn."

I asked Emily, "Do you want to come with me?"

I told you before that Emily was afraid of horses, and she knew that Sugar was in the barn. So she didn't want to go out there at first. She said, "I'll just wait in here until we're ready to leave."

"Oh, Emily," I said, "come on. Sugar won't hurt you. If you're going to be a soldier you have to be brave, right? I'll hold your hand if you want me to."

I put on my mittens and held out my hand to her. "Okay," she said. "I'll try not to get scared this time."

So Emily and I held hands and followed my mom out the door. In some places the snow was up to my knees. My dad had shoveled the driveway, and we followed his tracks in the snow to the side of the barn. When we walked inside, I couldn't believe my eyes.

"Wow!" I screamed.

My dad was leading Sugar out from his stall, and there was this big red sleigh in front of him in the middle of the barn. My dad built it by himself; and I guess it was supposed to be this Christmas present for the whole family, and for Sugar too, of course. My dad was grinning from ear to ear, like he was really proud of himself, and he said, "With all that snow piled up on the ground out there,

Rosie, you might want to ask Sugar to give you and Emily a ride into town."

Emily was still squeezing my hand pretty hard, but she didn't look like she was afraid anymore.

Sugar neighed and stamped the floor a couple of times, and then he walked past us and sort of sniffed at the two pink ribbons my dad had tied to the reins of the sleigh. Sugar looked over at me, and then all of a sudden he shook his head up and down. I told my mom and dad, "Sugar says this sleigh looks like the biggest toe shoe he's ever seen!"